UNBOUND

UNBOUND

He must be released for a little while

Ω

J.B. SIMMONS

For Jamison, Eliza, and any others to come

Ω

My name is Elijah Goldsmith. This is my story, and it's the honest-to-god truth. I'll tell you what I saw, what I felt, and that's about all I can do. You're probably going to ask me why it happened. I'll go ahead and tell you—I don't know. I figure nobody knows, nobody human anyway. Maybe you'll ask me how I know it's true. We'll get to that, but let's start with the dream. The dream, the agency, and then the girl...

1

I stood in the piazza facing St. Peter's Basilica in Rome. Bodies pressed around me and a pope's voice boomed in my ears. The ground began to tremble, as if aching under the crowd's weight. The cobblestones lurched under my feet. I staggered, tripped over someone, and fell flat on my back. People started running and screaming.

The sky darkened like nothing I'd ever seen. Lightning rolled through black clouds that were not there a moment before. A bolt struck the center of the piazza, hitting the cross atop the towering obelisk. The thunderclap was deafening. The obelisk tilted and fell, taking the cross down with it. Just as it crashed on the ground, the piazza split open—as if a giant had grabbed the colonnades on either side and ripped them apart. Hundreds of people plummeted into the chasm as I scrambled away to the piazza's far edge.

The splitting earth spread to the Basilica. Spider-web cracks splintered over the dome. The ancient stone groaned, swayed, and then imploded on itself. An enormous cloud of dust and debris billowed out into the chaos.

Then a shape rose from the chasm. Where the obelisk had been, a creature hovered low in the sky. It was like a dragon, but no storybook dragon. Ribbons of shadow and smoke coiled and danced around its long, slender form. Above its sentient face, onyx horns the size of trees stabbed into the sky. Its wings covered the entire width of the piazza.

A man walked toward the creature and paused at the chasm's edge. The creature fixed its red eyes on him as if seeing an old friend. He was a stunning man, with a flawless face and dark hair to his shoulders. His gray suit showed no blemish or wrinkle, despite the wind and the chaos. I knew him, but I could not name him. I couldn't say anything. I couldn't move. I could only *feel* the blackness, *feel* the end. It had to end.

And then it did. I woke up covered in sweat.

This was three nights in a row. Three nights of the same stupid nightmare. It had come from nowhere. I'd never even been to Rome.

I sat up, rubbed my eyes, and ran my hands through my hair. Today of all days, I could not have these visions in my head. Maybe I would try the new pill. If it let me control my dreams as they promised, I'd program my mind for more productive nights. I'd dream of breaking a code to stop the next attack on America, while finding a smart girl who'd appreciate it. That's what I needed: a smart girl, not a freakin' dragon.

I activated my precept's morning report. The four screens projected in my vision, showing it was 6:33 am, January 4, 2066. There were no major attacks last night. No news of Rome or of dragons.

I had seven minutes until my wake-up alarm, but I started my morning routine anyway. Thirty seconds in the shower chamber, one minute to slip on my black suit, and then my food arrived. Real eggs and coffee. My mouth watered. There had been too many mornings of pills and smoothies. This was a day for real food. I took my time with each bite while watching the video briefings.

The news focused on Iran again. The Persian nation had bought another piece of desert, while its leader denounced the United Nations for buying another robotics company. Apparently Iran didn't like the UN drones saving starving kids in Africa and trying to grow plants in the south Asia wastelands. But it didn't matter much, because China and the U.S. approved. Drones were as American as apple pies and precepts. Another briefing showed officials rounding up more fanatics who would not comply with the new global precept mandate.

These people were so weird. Precepts had been around long enough now. Besides, who would turn down a standard implant to be smarter, sharper, stronger? I called my precept "V." She was far from standard. She was the best my dad's money could buy, and he could buy anything.

Life without V would be like earth without the sun.

One of the screens drew my attention. It was a video of the police hauling a fanatic into a van. The man was holding a cross and flapping insanely, as if he had wings. I lifted my hand for V to raise the volume. The man was yelling something about an earthquake and a dragon from a pit. As the police slammed the van's door shut, I heard the man's last word: Rome.

My mouth fell open. No way *that* guy had seen what I'd seen. It was just a dream. I shuddered and shut off the screens.

"Order for delivery tonight," I told V. "Research report on dream pills, and a sample of three leading brands."

I finished the last of my eggs and downed the coffee. I stepped to the closet. V suggested the red, white, and blue tie, so I put it on. I walked out and left the hotel.

The sky was clear over the nation's capital. It would have been frigid back at school, but D.C.'s shield kept it warm. That shield and every other defense could soon be my responsibility.

This would be my first day as a spy.

"Y'all enjoy that hotel?" the instructor asked. "Last time you'll stay in one of those, as long as you're on duty with us." He looked like a cruise director with his pressed white suit and floppy brown hair, but he sounded like a southern plantation owner brought to the future. Strange choice for a spy.

A spinning holograph of the White House appeared before him. "You know," he said, "the President used to live in this house a few blocks from here."

Laughter rolled through our class. There were fifty of us in the room, and most looked like old bureaucrats.

"I know, I know, hard to imagine," he joked. "The President, living out in the open like that, with everyone knowing where he was? Well, life changes when you have power and responsibility. The world is watching, and it's our job to watch the world. Starting today, you used to stay in hotels, just like the President used to live in the White House."

The holograph blinked off.

"My name is Wade Brown, and I'll be your orientation leader. First, it is my honor to congratulate and welcome you. The International Security Agency is our greatest hope for a brighter future. We at ISA work under the United Nation's oversight to preserve what peace remains in the world and to protect against all acts of aggression."

He pointed to a man leaning by the door with his arms crossed. "This is Alexi Markos, our UN liaison. He's here to make sure our American division follows protocol." Mr. Brown grinned at the liaison, who nodded back with a shady smile.

"But I bet y'all know all this," the instructor said. "You're the best and brightest. You come from all walks of life. We have some rising stars"—he motioned in my table's direction—"and we have veterans of war. We're all here to serve, to do our part. So shall we get into the orienting?" The instructor pulled out a handkerchief and wiped sweat from his forehead. "We'll start with something near and dear to our hearts, HR! I'll cover benefits and retirement planning. Benefits start with health care, right? We have fourteen government policies to choose from. First…"

People began taking notes as the instructor talked. Notes! On tablets, no less. One grizzled man even used paper, writing by hand. Maybe these people were so old they didn't know how to use their precepts to record what the instructor said. V would remember every word for me, so I tuned Mr. Brown out. Besides, I'd figured we would start with our mission statement and a few things only ISA agents could know. Like the latest precept advances or some secret cloning program. I was starting to think I'd shown up in the wrong place.

Nothing about the room was what I'd expected. We were in groups of five around wooden tables. In the center of each table was an old-fashioned card with a number—"ISA-1," "ISA-2," and so on. I hadn't sat at a table without a screen or plug-ins since preschool. This was supposed to be the center of government intelligence, but it seemed more like a meeting room in a roadside motel. I would probably never set foot inside a motel, so this was as close as I'd get. Was this really how they'd treat the elite student fellows like me? I doubted it.

I might have walked out if not for the four others sitting at my table. They looked sharp, and we were the youngest in the room by far. "ISA-7" was written on our table's card and on each of our nametags.

Beside me was Charles. We were in the same class at my boarding school. He was already a legend at hacking, so it wasn't much of a surprise for him to be a student fellow. He wore black-rimmed glasses even though he could have seen just fine with lenses like mine. He'd told me girls digged glasses. Old school, he'd said. Today he was watching a movie on his glasses while pretending to listen to the instructor. From my angle, I could see most of what he could. It looked like a Kung Fu movie in Chinese. One of the fighters had a dragon emblazoned on his shirt. My thoughts flicked to my dream, but I forced it away.

My eyes caught the nametag of the other boy at our table: Patrick O'Grady. He had a blond crewcut and looked like he should be on a football field, not working in intelligence. Instead of a suit, he'd worn a short-sleeved shirt with a high, straight collar. It was only a little intimidating that the shirt's fabric stretched thin around his muscled biceps. From the size of him, I guessed he was a couple years older, probably in college already.

The other two at the table were girls, about my age. The dark-skinned one was Aisha Mahdi. She was a pretty Persian, with long black hair and dark almond eyes. On her brow was a thin, silver-colored diadem. I couldn't tell if it was connected to her brain as a precept enhancement, or if she was some kind of princess. I decided her petulant lips made her look like royalty.

The last girl was, well, she was different—like a golden sunrise is different. She had honey blond curls, freckles, and skin the color of café au lait. She looked like she was actually listening to the instructor. Her nametag said Naomi Parish and, unlike the rest of ours, it had a red star drawn after her name. I had no idea what that meant. But I wanted to know.

I looked up and found Naomi smiling at me. I felt my cheeks heating when I smiled back, and I told myself it was only because she'd caught me staring at her nametag...on her chest. I turned back towards the instructor.

"If you walk away with only one thing," Mr. Brown was

saying, "you must remember ISA.you.gov. It has all the information we covered and more. It has a live chat for questions. So tag that site with your precepts. For you old timers out there, favorite it in your watches, phones, and tablets." Half the room laughed, the grey-haired half. "We'll get you using upgraded precepts soon enough. For now, just remember, ISA.you.gov."

"Okay," he continued, clasping his hands, "that's it for the HR basics. This afternoon I'll start letting you in on some secret stuff. No, we haven't sent anyone to Mars, and yes, we still use carbon fuels. As y'all know, we've been too busy with wars and natural disasters to live up to all the predictions for the twenty-first century. But, thanks to those wars, we've gotten very, *very* good at surveillance. More on that to come! Now we have our first breakout sessions. Check the map on the screens to find your room."

As the room began to stir, the instructor looked towards my table with a Cheshire-cat grin. "ISA-7!" he said, waving for us to come to him. "You won't see your group listed. Y'all are coming with me."

3

"Hope y'all found my talk helpful." The instructor glanced back over his shoulder as he led us out of the room. "I try to liven it up, you know, because orientations can be boring."

When he looked forward again, Charles caught my attention and laughed silently, pointing at Mr. Brown. The morning could not have been more boring. I smiled at Charles, but for some reason it didn't seem funny. The instructor's easy demeanor was *too* easy—like he was hiding something.

We walked past an elevator bank to a door under an exit sign. The instructor pressed his palm to a panel on the wall. A green light flashed, and the door swung open. We followed him into a dimly lit stairwell. A rush of cool air greeted us as we entered. I peered down the gap at the center of the stairwell and could see only darkness below.

No bottom was in sight. I was the last of our group to begin heading down.

"Mr. Brown?" asked Naomi after one flight of stairs.

"Yes?" he said, without slowing.

"This building's records indicate only one floor below ground." She spoke with calm precision. That was smart—checking the floor plans. V could have done that, if I'd thought of it. "And my precept's signal is growing weak," she continued. "We may lose connection if we go much further. Where are you taking us?"

Mr. Brown laughed off her concern. "Already asking questions, huh! That's why we pick you star students. We're heading to a secret spot. It's very cool. You'll see soon enough." He paused for a moment and looked up at Naomi. "And, please, call me Wade."

He turned and kept walking down.

Naomi glanced back at me and shrugged. I wanted to say something witty, but nothing came. Where was V with a quip when I needed it? V's focus seemed elsewhere. She was upping my adrenalin and magnifying my vision slightly. I wasn't sure what to make of Wade, but I wasn't going to back out now. This was closer to what I'd expected. Maybe our ISA-7 group was heading to the real training and the real secrets.

As we wound our way down the stairs, I could not pull my eyes away from Naomi. She was lean and tall, with a glide to her steps. Her fitted white pants and blue dress shirt were well worn, almost like they were from a thrift shop. But her sleeves were folded back casually, confidently, the same way the girls from our sister boarding school wore their designer shirts. I don't know why, but I really liked her style.

"How much longer?" Charles asked Wade after we'd gone down five or six flights. "Don't they make elevators for this?"

"Almost there!" Wade shouted up.

A few moments later we stopped in front of a door. I peered down the gap at the center of the stairwell again. There was still no bottom in sight.

"Come on now, Elijah," Wade beckoned.

I walked through the door and Wade followed last. The door shut behind us and clicked. A red light blinked on the panel beside the door's handle. My internet connection was suddenly gone. V went into local mode, so I lost access to the outside world. It made my shoulders tense.

Wade took the lead again, walking down a hallway ten feet wide and about a million feet long. Plain grey metal doors were on both sides every twenty steps or so. Fluorescent lights flickered on the ceiling. No one had made lights like those in fifty years.

I fell into step beside Naomi at the back of the group.

"Naomi, right?" I asked.

"Yes." She leaned closer as we walked and stared down at my chest. Then she smiled at me accusingly. "Good thing for these nametags. So you're Elijah?"

I felt my cheeks flushing again. "My friends call me Eli. Where are you from?"

"North Carolina, mostly. You?"

"New York, but I'm in school in Massachusetts. You know, for a southerner, you don't have much of an accent, unlike our instructor." I nodded up ahead, where Wade was chatting with Aisha.

"My dad's a missionary." She fingered a gold cross hanging from a red ribbon necklace. "We traveled a lot growing up."

"That must have been fun. My dad's a banker. *He* traveled a lot. He brought me some super souvenirs."

She smiled. "A touch bitter?"

"Maybe a little," I confessed, grinning back. Her smiling face made me feel light and innocent. "Where have you traveled?"

Before she could answer, Patrick's loud voice interrupted us. "Look man," he was saying to Wade, "you seem like a nice guy, but I don't like this. Where are you taking us?" Patrick had grabbed Wade's arm and made him stop. We were about halfway to the hall's other end.

Wade kept smiling, or maybe he sneered. "I know it seems strange, but we're just going to a different building for the next session, and it's faster to get there this way. Soon you'll know all these secret passages." He winked at us. "Come on, we're getting close."

He pulled his arm away from Patrick, smoothed his sleeve, and walked on at a casual pace. It was not much further before we stopped in front of another plain door.

"Here we are," Wade announced as he pressed his palm on another panel. Again a green light blinked, but the door did not open.

Wade turned to us and this time there was no smile. He suddenly looked nothing like a cruise director. "You have much to learn," he said. "Watch."

He leaned toward the door and then stuck his face *into* it. The metal bent like wet clay, molding to the shape of his face. He pulled back, leaving his face's impression in the metal.

The ceiling suddenly slid apart. Dozens of androids dropped down beside us. They started striking like snakes.

Adrenalin-fueled instinct took over. I jumped over a robot's swinging arm, then jerked away from another. As I turned to run, I glimpsed a metallic blur sweep Charles's legs out from under him.

I sprinted off, with Naomi running at my side.

We'd taken only a few strides when more androids dropped in the hallway before us. There were too many, too fast. I dodged one, only for another to catch my heel and send me crashing to the floor. Naomi went down beside me. Lifeless robotic eyes surrounded us. One of the androids plunged a needle into my shoulder. I felt it injecting something.

As everything faded to black, I managed to look to my other side. The last thing I saw was Naomi's ashen, freckled face.

4

"You have been unconscious for thirty minutes, but you could just as easily be dead." It was Wade's voice. He had lost all trace of a warm, southern accent.

My eyelids lifted slowly. I was in a huge, bright room. Sunlight streamed through a wall of windows that looked over the Potomac River and the Washington Monument. All five of us from the ISA-7 table were tied to chairs. Naomi was in the chair to my right. Three men were standing beside Wade, staring at us. Wade was still dressed like a cruise director. The others wore plain grey jumpsuits.

"You're in the Pentagon," said one of the men.

I blinked three times, trying to bring up V. Nothing came. They had somehow shut down my precept. I tried to stay calm, but I was close to freaking out. Was this really training? What were they going to do to us?

"You think you know why you're here," another man

said, stepping closer, appraising us. "You think you're special, but I'll tell you now, you're nothing but meat on a chopping block until you learn to observe like a spy. That's why I'm here." The man was older, maybe fifty, with a bald head half covered by a thin circuit board. His round body and face looked about as friendly as a boulder. "If you all pass the entrance exam, you five will be a team. You might as well get to know one another."

He approached Patrick to my left.

"What is this?" demanded Patrick. "I came here to be an ISA fellow, to train as a spy but then get back to my life." He glanced at the rest of us. "I figure we all did."

"That's right," agreed Aisha. "I have four years before my commitment begins." She looked down at the bindings around her wrists. "If you call this training, I want out."

The man's stern gaze was locked on Aisha. "So you thought you'd show up for a week, collect your ISA resume line, and head back to your life unchanged?"

"No, it's not like that," Aisha protested. "But I didn't come here to be attacked and tied up."

The man glanced at the rest of us. "Anyone else?"

No one spoke. It was a unique honor to be invited as an ISA fellow, and prior fellows had gone on to do big things. I figured we all knew there'd be some surprises. We also knew about the commitment. It was a one-year minimum for me, after college. It was probably similar for all of us. In return, they'd teach us the secrets of spying and the best technologies. I wanted to do my part, to serve, and to prove wrong everyone who thought a rich kid like me would just flit his life away. But still, why'd they tie us up? It looked like I was not alone in thinking we'd have an easier start than this.

The man held his hand up to his ear, as if to amplify a sound. "That's what I like to hear—silent obedience. Here's a first lesson. Spying is never a part-time job. Now, where were we? Ah yes, getting to know each other. This will all go better if you stay quiet and listen."

He stepped up to Patrick and stared hard at him. "Patrick O'Grady thinks he's here because he's a good ole boy—as smart and strong as they come. In every year of high school, he won the Texas scholar athlete award. He proudly helps out the wimps in his class. He's heading to Stanford next year with a full-ride to play quarterback." The man leaned forward, within inches of Patrick's face. "The ISA needs studs like you, right Patrick?"

Patrick met his stare evenly but did not answer. The man stepped back and blinked. An almost life-size 3D image of our group appeared beside him.

"Let's see how Patrick handled this first test, shall we?"

The image started to move, lifelike. It showed all of us walking down the long hall behind Wade. It showed Patrick grabbing Wade's arm, trying to stop him, but then following on. I wondered how they had gotten such clear footage of us. I hadn't noticed a single camera.

"Patrick sensed something was wrong," the man said. "That's good. That's necessary. But you must learn to act! Trying to act is not enough. You must act and *affect* what is around you." He pointed at Patrick with his thumb up, like a gun. "Patrick could have saved your group, but he failed. One down." He pretended to shoot Patrick with his hand.

Then he turned to Aisha. "Aisha Mahdi, our Persian princess, born in the U.S.A. She thinks she's here because of her beauty, culture, and wit. And she really is a princess in Iran, where she'll be returning this year as the youngest-ever Iranian graduate of Harvard. Will your royalty save you when a stranger leads you down a dangerous path? Let's see."

The image beside the man shifted and began to move again. It zoomed in on Aisha and Wade. They were both smiling widely and laughing. She reached over and clasped Wade's shoulder fondly. The image paused, showing her happy, gorgeous face.

"Trying to win the favor of your instructor?" asked the man. "That's all well and good. You can seduce to succeed, but you must never trust." The man pointed to the frozen image of Aisha before us. "This is a face of trust. Trust no one!"

"Let me go!" she snapped back, trying to wrest her wrists free. "Who do you think you are?"

"Our enemies can be anyone, anywhere, any time." The man's voice went stoic. "They litter the country where you'll be going, my dear Aisha. Be thankful for my lessons. Without them you will die. With them you might live a little longer."

The man's head swiveled to Charles. "Charles Chang, Chinese American *par excellence*."

As the man stepped closer to him, Charles began

straining against the bindings of his chair. They didn't budge.

"Good, Charles, good. I bet you can guess why we picked you. You're as gifted a hacker as we've seen. And you're a fighter, a multilingual tiger in a cage. But do you know the tiger's greatest weakness?"

Charles had gone still. "An unbound tiger would rip open your throat," he said calmly, "so I guess we tigers lack restraint…except when you tie us down."

Anger flashed in the man's eyes. He pointed to the circuit on his head. "Do I need to remind you what we can do if we hack into your precept?"

Charles shook his head.

"Good. I'll ask again," the man said. "Do you know the tiger's greatest weakness?"

"Arrogance," Charles growled.

"Precisely," the man replied. "The master of the jungle does not know his weaknesses. They are not weaknesses of physical strength or cunning, but of failing to detect dangers. Let's watch a tiger and see."

The image now showed Charles outside the elevator bank, before we went down the stairs, joking with me about Wade's boring orientation. Then the image shifted and showed Charles walking down the hall beside Patrick. While the tall quarterback wore a look of growing trepidation, Charles was laughing again. The image stopped but the sound of Charles's laughing continued.

"Arrogance," the man said over the sound, "leads even the fiercest and sharpest of tigers into a false sense of security. We must never be arrogant in our line of work."

The man's gaze turned toward me. As he approached, my spine went rigid. The man's pale blue eyes made me feel cold.

"Elijah, Elijah. Enjoying your winter break?"

I kept my face blank, as I had from the start.

"You think you're unique," he said, "because of your brilliance, your pedigree, and your connections? Your rich father bought you every genetic enhancement, along with one of the best precepts in the world. But you can't buy what it takes to survive. You think it'll be cool to play a spy while you're a freshman at Princeton, with your buddy Charles? I think you'll be lucky to live that long. Watch."

The image returned. It showed me in the stairwell, walking down after Naomi and staring at her. A red line appeared on the image, following my line of sight and connecting it with Naomi's back. The image moved at double-speed while I walked down the stairs. The red line moved with me, showing how my gaze stayed locked on Naomi. The image then shifted to us in the hall. It zoomed onto my face as I talked to Naomi. It showed the color in my cheeks, the excitement in my eyes. The image froze there, focused on my flushed face.

"I'll spare you the embarrassment of showing your heart rate in that moment," the man said. "Passion can be a useful tool, but it is usually a distraction, a lethal distraction. We must harness our passions." His pale eyes fixed on me.

I'd seen enough to not try talking back. "Yes," I answered, "and, I'm sorry, but I did not catch your name."

He smiled for the first time I'd seen—a devilish and frightful snarl. "No, you did not *catch* my name, because I did not throw it. Work with me another year, and then I might let you know my initials. Until then, you can call me Captain." He sighed, like a disappointed teacher. "Now Elijah, passion and curiosity, these are tools. You must never let them control you. Use them. Do not be used by them."

The man turned last to Naomi. She was completely still in her seat. Her face was smooth and relaxed, with a grin playing on her lips.

"Naomi Parish, you think you're here because it's God's will for your life." The man suddenly laughed. "I know it's true you believe that, so pardon my skepticism. You're really here because you have more talent than the rest of this group combined, even though you're the youngest. A half dozen languages, beautiful composure, unparalleled IQ, and wise beyond your years—those are the makings of a spy. So what did you do wrong? Here we go."

The image tracked Naomi walking past the elevator bank and through the stairwell door. She wore a look of confusion and uncertainty. The image paused.

"See," the man said, speaking to the rest of us, "Naomi knew. She sensed that Wade was leading you towards danger. She was the first to detect something amiss. There is no greater gift for a spy. But keep watching."

The image replayed Naomi's brief conversation with Wade inside the stairwell. It showed his warm response, and then it showed her look of concern lifting. She followed after him and the image dissipated.

"You had faith in Wade!" the Captain scoffed. "Why?"

"I had no reason to question him," Naomi answered.

"You had every reason! You always have every reason. Question everyone. Question Jesus Christ if the dead man haunts your work." A look of indignation passed over Naomi's face, but the Captain had already moved on.

He addressed all of us. "This is your first lesson, a lesson on instincts. You must make these five instincts part of your very soul." He held up his thick pointer finger and spoke like Moses issuing commandments. "First, act and affect what is around you. Second, trust no one. Third, never let pride obscure danger. Fourth, use passion only as a tool. Fifth, question everything."

He held his hand up high, with his five fingers stretched out. "These five things will keep you alive in a lethal world." He closed his hand into a fist. "We must work together to survive. We must survive to succeed. And we must succeed if our world is to enjoy any peace."

The Captain saluted us and blinked slowly. The floor panel under his feet began to drop, lowering him out of the room. And just like that, he was gone.

"Sorry about tying you up," said Wade. "Rough introduction, I know. We've all gone through it. You're the world's most promising talents, and our goal is to make you even better. We're going to let you go now, but while you stretch, let me offer a few last thoughts for the day."

The cords around us suddenly released, as if dropped from a magnet. My body was stiff as I stood.

"I really am Wade Brown," he continued, "y'all really can call me Wade, and my accent is real. I'm from south Georgia, even if I hide it sometimes. We all hide something for the sake of duty. You're gonna face more tests here this week, but I'll be here for the full ride. You can trust me as much as anyone. Any questions?"

"Who was that man?" Patrick asked.

"The Captain?" Wade said. "He's a veteran, a spy who's survived more than a cat with nine lives. He's been leading this training for a decade. You'll be getting to know him better. Anything else?"

"What was that circuit on the Captain's head?" Charles asked. "Some enhanced version of a precept?"

"Good question," Wade said. "The short answer is yes, and you'll learn more if you stick around. Tomorrow, report to the base of the Washington Monument at 5 am, unless of course, you decide ISA-7 is not for you. Hope to see y'all there."

5

"You were checking her out," Charles ribbed again as we waited in the hotel lobby. Naomi, Aisha, and Patrick were joining us soon for dinner.

"No," I said, "I already told you. I was just watching my step going down the stairs."

"Checking her out." He grabbed my shoulder and pretended to look serious. "Look man, I'm not saying she's not worth it. She's smoking hot. Pretty face, lean body, some spark. And I know you like freckles. There's no one like her at our sister schools, that's for sure."

I was shaking my head. "She's interesting, that's all Charles."

"Oh, she's interesting all right. I'm just saying you better own up to it, because our pal Patrick has eyes for her, too. You boys can fight it out. Aisha's more my style." He pressed his palms together and flashed a devious grin.

"We Asians will stick like wet rice."

"She's Iranian, Charles."

"She's a fox, Eli."

We laughed together. Charles was always saying something ridiculous. We'd never been too close at school, but now that we were both joining ISA-7 and heading to Princeton in the fall, we'd be spending plenty of time together. I could think of worse company.

"So what do you make of Patrick?" I asked, trying to change the subject away from Naomi. "Why'd he suggest this dinner?"

"He's a Texan." Charles shrugged as if that explained everything. "A quarterback's gotta lead the team and date the cheerleaders, right?"

"I'm guessing there's more to it than that. Remember what the Captain said," I copied his stern voice, "question everyone."

"The Captain's full of smoke," Charles said. "I'm sure he'll teach us a few things, but I don't like his style. Anyway, yeah, Patrick definitely gives me some questions. You really think he's fit for ISA-7? He seems too straight-laced to be a spy. Why would he want to join, anyway?"

"I doubt anyone turns down the ISA fellowship. Besides, he's probably the strongest and fastest of our group. Maybe we're the brains, he's the brawn."

"Brawn is so last century," Charles said. "Maybe it's because he's Catholic."

"So?" I asked.

"Think about the five of us fellows. They've got the

major religions covered: a Pope lover, a Jesus freak, a Jew," he nodded to me, "a Muslim, and an atheist." He pointed to himself.

"Missing a couple, but I guess so," I said. It still didn't make sense why ISA would care about the religions of its spies. Maybe we'd be posted to places where our backgrounds would help us blend in. "Do you think we'll stay together in the field, or are we just in the training together?"

"I've heard they let in ten fellows like us each year," Charles answered. "Maybe they keep us in pockets of five. Who knows?"

"I know!" Patrick's voice was right beside my ear. I jumped in surprise. I never heard him coming.

"Sorry guys, just proving a point," he said. "Even a Catholic Texan might surprise you with what he can do."

"I didn't mean that," Charles said, "I mean, I'm sure you have what it takes if you've been invited to ISA-7."

Patrick smiled in response, looming over us by at least half a foot. He put his arms over our shoulders, pulling us into a huddle. I felt like a paper doll in his strong grip.

"We're in this together, gentlemen," he whispered. "We each contribute to our team. We have to work as one if we hope to serve our country well." He released us, stepped back, and made the sign of the cross. "God willing," he continued, "we might just be the ones to save the world from whatever threat is coming next." Charles was right. Patrick seemed way too vanilla to be a spy.

"You boys already scheming against us?" Naomi's

voice was like a rush of warm wind in my ears. She walked up with Aisha at her side. They were a stunning pair. "Ready for dinner?"

"Absolutely," Patrick said, with a big goofy grin toward Naomi. "This place is awesome. It's called Luz. They scan your chip when you walk in the door. Then, whatever your body needs most, that's what they serve you. Come on, it's not far from here."

Patrick roped Naomi into conversation as he led us out of the hotel. I walked beside Charles while he flirted with Aisha.

The capital's streets were brighter than day under the white lights shining from every building. The lights formed stripes with the lines of lush green plants climbing the buildings' walls. We weaved through crowds of people rushing about. Their eyes looked ahead, but they were distant, focused on watching or reading whatever their precepts were showing them.

It was not long before Patrick stopped outside a new-looking restaurant. We walked in after him.

The android greeter directed us to a booth. I slipped in front of Charles and Aisha, securing my spot beside Naomi before we sat down. Patrick was on her other side. Charles flashed me a knowing smile from across the table.

A few minutes later our food came out of a panel by the booth's wall. The plate set before me had a bare salmon fillet, a pile of raw kale, and three odd-shaped mushrooms. Naomi's plate had a small chunk of steak and a beet salad. Everyone was given water and a stack of pills.

"Cool, huh?" Patrick said, as he poked at his salmon and zucchini. "Last time I was here they served me an avocado and a stack of blackberries. Of course, we all get the pills." He held up a small clear capsule. "These are the best on the market."

"I like it," Aisha said. "If the Captain were here, I'm guessing they'd give him a plate full of prunes. The man needs to lighten up."

We laughed and dug into the food. Halfway through the meal, I saw my opening to pull Naomi into a side chat. She turned slightly in my direction as she brought her glass of water to her lips. I caught her eyes and smiled.

"This morning," I said, "you were going to tell me where you traveled growing up."

"Oh, was I?" She set her glass down gently. "Something must have interrupted us."

"I hate it when that happens. So…you lived abroad?"

She nodded. "Didn't we all? You lived in Jerusalem for two years."

I started to ask her how she knew it but stopped short. Of course her precept could have tracked that down. My excitement about her looking me up outweighed my frustration that I had not yet done the same for her. Shame on V for letting me get lost in news and messages in the short time before dinner. And too bad looking up Naomi while talking to her would be a major social faux pas. It was time to get creative.

"Notice anything else about my profile?" I asked.

Her eyes looked into mine as if she were dissecting a

frog. "Your family and schooling make you privileged," her voice dropped so only I could hear, "but I think you're running from all that. Rich boys from Manhattan don't join the ISA. You've got too much to lose. Why are you here?"

My mouth had fallen open. She could've gotten those facts from public data, but she couldn't have read my intentions anywhere. I was starting to like this girl.

Keep it cool, I told myself. "The Captain said you were the best of us. Why is that?" I nodded to the others at the table, who were talking about the drone missions in South America. Their plates were almost empty.

Naomi opened her mouth to speak, but hesitated.

"I'll offer you a trade," I said. "Interested?" My feet were bouncing under the table, but I kept my face calm.

"Let me guess," she said. "We tell each other why we're here?"

"No, I wouldn't dare ask for so much so soon." I held her gaze, thinking hard. What would a good southern girl want from me right now? I had an idea. "You let me buy you ice cream after this, and then I'll tell you why I'm here."

Her lips curled into a curious smile. "Ice cream?"

"I know, old school. You like butter pecan?" It was a hunch.

She nodded, her smile wavering almost imperceptibly. "You're full of surprises, Elijah. Fine, I'll let you buy me ice cream."

"So it's a deal?" I asked.

"Deal."

"Cookies and cream," she placed her order and turned to me with a grin. "Sometimes I stray from my favorites."

"Butter pecan," I ordered, holding my wrist to the scanner to pay.

Our cones showed up a moment later. We took them and walked outside. The streets were emptier now that the city's lights had dimmed for the night. We found a bench beside a fountain in a park. The grass, flowers, and trees had the sheen of plants in a greenhouse.

"Have you been to the museum?" I pointed to the White House at the far end of the park.

"Yes, it's great." She crossed her legs and took a lick of ice cream. "You?"

"Nah. My dad knew the past couple Presidents. He's a big donor, so I've gotten to meet them, too. I figure that's better than learning from a museum."

"You might be surprised," she said without a trace of being impressed. "You know, after dinner, you were a little rude to Patrick."

"What?" The abrupt subject change made me miss slightly as I took my next lick. I thought she hadn't heard me talking to him.

"You have a little..." She pointed to my nose and laughed. She reached up and wiped off a drop of ice cream with her napkin. "Patrick," she said, "he wanted to join us for ice cream. You were rude to not invite him."

"He wasn't part of the deal." And, yeah, maybe I'd told that to Patrick with a touch of pride.

"Whatever you said made him look a little down," Naomi said. "We should be building each other up."

"Fair enough," I said, "but you wanted to know why I'm here, and I can't just tell everyone that."

"Why not?" Her open demeanor was disarming.

"Aren't we learning to be spies?" I asked.

"Spies are not what most people think. We don't have to hide everything. Be kind to Patrick. You never know when you might need him to return the favor. Okay?"

"Okay." This was not going as I'd planned. My confidence was being licked away as fast as her ice cream.

"So how about the other half of our deal?" she asked, her voice light again.

"The part where I tell you why I'm here?"

"Yes, that part."

"You seem to know a lot about me. What do you think?"

"That's not the deal. I want to hear it in your words." She bit off part of the cone. Her hair matched its honey color.

"Maybe it's fate," I said.

"Fate?"

"Yeah." I decided it was no use hiding my interest in her. "You know, some unseen pattern leading me to enjoy this ice cream with you."

"I doubt that," she said. "Besides, you can't believe in fate unless you believe in a higher power. Try again."

"Here's what I believe." I opted for something close to the truth. She seemed to bring it out of me. "Higher powers must be so high up that they forgot about mankind. The world is spiraling out of control. The wars are getting worse, disasters are everywhere, and most people are content to let the decay continue as long as they have full bellies and entertaining shows. We've got plenty of those where we live."

"I agree with you about the people, but not about the higher powers. You still didn't answer my question, though. Why you? Is it your fate to stop the decay?"

"Shouldn't that be everyone's fate?"

"Maybe it *should* be," she said, "but it's not. You have every reason not to join ISA. Your family's banking fortune awaits you. You have an elite education and a life of pleasure ahead. You could be shielded from the world's worst."

Her words were another version of the same story everyone was always telling me. The story I was going to prove wrong. "I never liked the easy path," I said. "It's too boring, too weak. By joining ISA, I get a chance to make a difference, to fight the decay, to become part of something bigger."

Her eyebrows lifted slightly. "Sounds impressive." She was clearly not convinced.

"I also think you exaggerate the risks," I continued. "Our group will have hardly any time in the field these first few years. We may be the chosen fellows, but we're still trainees. We go back to school in a week and leave this behind except for virtual work and occasional trainings."

"I doubt that, after what the Captain said." She studied me. "But you're still hiding something. What troubles you, Elijah?" Her doe eyes demanded honesty. She took the last bite of her cone.

"Not much, Naomi." I mocked her serious tone. "As you said, I have it all. Riches, status, dashing good looks." I smiled. "You forgot to say that last part."

She smiled back. "You're nice, and you might be handsome in the right light. But..." She pressed her eyes closed and held her hands out as if ready to catch a feather floating down in the space between us. She just sat there, saying nothing, eyes closed. This was getting awkward. I don't know why, but I reached out and put my hands in the air just above hers. I could have sworn there was energy there—between us. I lowered my hands until they just grazed hers.

She yanked her hands away. Her eyes opened wide. They blazed like a supernova about to gobble up a tiny, cold planet. "Something looms over you," she said, "like a shadow over your mind. Tell me what it is."

"No clue," I shrugged, "maybe my dreams?" The words slipped out, and I immediately wished I had them back.

"You have troubling dreams?"

I nodded.

"These dreams are unusual, maybe similar over time?"

I nodded again.

"What did you dream last night?"

Great. Apparently this pretty girl was a psychic. My dream was the last thing I wanted to share with her. No better way to win her over than to tell her I'd just had visions of a dragon destroying St. Peter's Basilica. I might as well have worn a sign saying, "freak approaching."

"Tell me, please," she said. "I promise I won't hold it against you."

"It was just a dream," I downplayed. "It doesn't matter."

"How about I make you another deal?" she asked.

"I like deals." Especially deals with her. The hair was standing up on the back of my neck. No one had ever put me on edge like this.

"You tell me your dream now, and I'll invite you on another date."

A date—she called it a date. I controlled my excitement and played it cool: "When?"

"This week. I choose the time and place."

"Done." Why not? I figured she was going to keep

prying until she learned about the dream anyway. I finished off my ice cream cone and organized my thoughts.

"Don't leave out any details, or the deal's off," she threatened. "I won't interrupt."

I nodded and began to tell her what I'd seen in the dream. St. Peter's Basilica, the huge crowd, the earthquake, and the lightning. I described the chaos and the dragon rising up from the abyss. I described the man, the stunning man who walked towards the dragon. I did not tell her how the dream made me feel. I did not mention my terror, but when I finished, her expression told me she knew.

"Thank you, Elijah." Her voice was steady and intense. "Wednesday night," she said, "after our training, let's meet here at 8. Let's keep this dream a secret from ISA-7, okay?"

"Sure," I said.

"Don't tell anyone, not even Charles. Got it?"

"Yeah." It's not like I was desperate to tell people a dragon visited my dreams at night.

She stood from the bench and reached her arms high in the air to stretch. Her long body had the elegance of a model on a catwalk. "Come on, let's get back to the hotel." She sounded almost playful again. "We have a long week ahead of us, if today was any indication."

We talked of little things on the short walk back, and then we parted in the lobby. No hug, no handshake. Just an awkward exchange of "goodnights."

As soon as I was back in my room, I asked V to run a report on Naomi. I changed clothes, brushed my teeth, popped a dream pill, and fell into bed. By then the report was ready.

Words, images, and videos began flashing through my lenses. I learned that Naomi came from a huge family. Her mom was a white southern belle. Her dad was a black basketball star who'd given away his money to serve the poor abroad. She had an older sister and four younger brothers. None of them were psychics, but they were all religious.

V flagged a series of odd gaps in the info about her family's faith. Public records showed membership in some megachurch, but left out details. The government required reporting on religious attendance and giving. That data was missing, even though the rest of the report seemed complete. It made me think of the video of that fanatic being hauled into a police van.

I shifted the focus to Naomi in particular. She had lived with her family in seven African countries, but spent the past four years home-schooled in North Carolina. For a decade, every picture had showed her wearing that golden cross necklace with the red ribbon.

It all screamed: *she's not your type!*

But then came the similarities. We were both Leos, born in the year of the dragon, on the exact same day: July 26, 2048. Her mom had died when she was eight, just like mine. She'd always been exceptional. In every group, she was the smartest, the most driven, the most successful— just like me. She'd won national competitions in both math and music. I'd won in science and debate. At sixteen, she'd just missed the U.S. Olympic team for the mile. And hey, last year I'd made my school's track team.

I honed in on one of the videos from the report. It showed Naomi dressed in a stunning black gown, singing solo before a packed music hall. I motioned for V to increase the volume. It was a song in French. Naomi's green eyes stared through the screen in bright, open beauty.

As I lay on my back in the hotel bed, Naomi was looking down at me, singing to me. Her voice was the most amazing I'd ever heard. I had V loop the video, and Naomi serenaded me to sleep.

Apparently the dream pill was a dud, because the dream came again, with the dragon and the man, for the fourth straight night. When I woke, drenched in sweat, V confirmed St. Peter's Basilica was still standing. I wished I could've said the same about myself. But the past day and night, between the dream, the training, and Naomi—especially Naomi—were making me stagger. Cracks were spreading through my foundations. Part of me feared I was swaying like the Basilica after the quake, just waiting for a knockout punch.

7

I pressed my hands against the cool, white stone and craned my neck back. The Washington Monument was not budging. It hadn't budged in ages. It just stood there, simple and straight as its namesake, while the city and the world buzzed around it in dizzying circles.

"Ever been to the top?" Patrick asked.

"Nope," said Charles.

"Me neither," answered Aisha.

"Only once," Naomi said, "when I was a little girl."

"Same here," Patrick added.

"You were a little girl?" Charles mocked.

"Very funny, Charles," Patrick said. "The view from up there is amazing. How about you, Eli? Been to the top?"

I pulled my gaze away from the obelisk and turned to the others. The four of them were staring at me. "Yeah, a few times," I said. "You think robots are going to spring out of the Monument to attack us now?"

"I doubt it," laughed Naomi. I smiled at her, pretending that her laugh didn't make my head spin.

"But something should have happened by now," Aisha said. "We've been here since 5, like Wade asked. The city's overnight curfew ends soon, so people will be about." She motioned around us, to the open space of the national mall. It would be at least an hour before the first light of day, but spotlights around the monuments made the mall glow in the predawn mist. There was a slight chill in the air. Not even the city's shield could keep it balmy in January. "How long are we going to have to wait here?" Aisha asked.

"I don't know," Patrick said. "Maybe they want us to get to know each other better."

"What's left to learn?" asked Charles. "The Captain told us the basics, and last night I learned Patrick needed zucchini. Plus, by now we've all run reports on each other, right?"

An awkward silence followed, with each of us avoiding the others' eyes. Of course we'd run the reports. Maybe I'd spent a lot more time on Naomi's, but I'd squeezed in Aisha's and Patrick's this morning. The ISA wouldn't have picked us if we weren't the type to do our homework.

"You might be right," Naomi eventually said, "but even the best minds and precepts can miss the full story. Not everything can be gleaned from public data."

Her mysterious tone begged me to pry further, as did the missing info from her report. "What's not public these days?" I asked in an innocent tone.

"How about thoughts, beliefs, and *dreams*?" Naomi held my gaze.

"Oh, those things are not as safe as you think," Charles said. "They're not public, but I bet when we link our precepts with the ISA network, they can hack in and learn more than we'd like."

"What do you mean?" Patrick asked. He glanced furtively at Naomi, then back to Charles. Had something passed between them? "There's no way they can know what we believe just because our precepts link to their network."

"Patrick's right," Aisha chimed in. "Beliefs require more than the mind. I think what Charles means is that, whenever you link your precept to a network, there's a risk your incoming and outgoing precept data will be compromised. So whatever you've sent or received through your precept could be hacked into. Right, Charles?"

"Exactly," he said. "Precepts are playgrounds for hackers like me. And think about it, is there anything you think or do without transmitting data through your precept?"

"Yeah, I'm a purist with dental hygiene," I deadpanned, "so I shut down my precept when I brush my teeth."

"Smart move," laughed Charles. "That means you can think whatever you want for one minute a day. But for me, well, I don't take a breath without my precept. I prefer not to live with an animal brain."

"It's not like that," Naomi objected. "We don't *need* precepts. We wouldn't even have them if the human mind lacked the spark of creation. Precepts are just our newest tools."

"But some tools change everything," Charles said.

"Hey," Patrick interrupted, "what's that?" He was pointing to something zooming toward us over the mall's long reflecting pool.

"A drone." Charles's eyes grew distant, as if engaged with his precept. "It's for us."

Sure enough, a moment later the melon-sized drone was hovering beside our group. It looked like a standard shipping drone—a mini helicopter with blades spinning so fast it could carry packages ten times its weight.

"Good morning, folks," said Wade's voice from the little chopper. "Press your wrists to the drone. You each have instructions for this exercise."

Charles reached forward without hesitation. The rest of us followed his lead. Our five arms were like spokes connecting to the drone in the middle.

Patrick is your partner. I suddenly heard the message in my mind, in V's voice. *You have seven minutes to touch Lincoln's feet in his Memorial. Don't let ANYTHING stop you.* The words stopped.

I glanced at Patrick.

"Lincoln?" he asked. "Seven minutes?"

I nodded. "Let's go."

The others still standing there as we took off running down the slight hill toward the Lincoln Memorial. I had V do a quick check for me—the Memorial was one mile away. If I'd known they were going to make me sprint a mile in under seven minutes, maybe I would've done some warming up.

It took everything I had to keep up with Patrick. His fast, gliding paces looked like a smooth jog. V showed we were beating the speed we needed to make it in time. We were about halfway there, just reaching the path beside the reflecting pool, when Patrick slowed slightly.

"Look!" he shouted, pointing overhead.

The drone zoomed past us with Charles and Aisha hanging from it. They flew low over the water and dropped off at the pool's far end. I slowed my jog to watch where they'd go from there. Where was Naomi?

"Come on! Faster!" Patrick urged. "They may be trying to stop us. I'll run ahead to make sure all's clear." His long legs wheeled like a cheetah's as he raced forward. I sprinted as fast as I could, but there was no way I could equal his strides. If there was any dust on this path, he'd left me in it.

I was nearing the end of the reflecting pool, within two minutes of the Memorial, when I heard a loud splash to my right, just behind me.

Then came a scream. It sounded like Naomi.

Water was flying everywhere by the pool's edge. Suddenly Naomi's head sprang up out of the water. "Elijah!"

Something yanked her down again. No more splashes. She was completely underwater.

Lincoln's feet could wait. I charged over and saw her terrified face blurred by the churning ripples. Her body was flat against the pool's bottom, writhing helplessly against two cords that tied her down at the legs and the chest. No one else was around.

I dashed into the shallow water and pulled at one of the cords. It was tight and strong as a chain. *Don't panic*, I told myself. I jerked at the other cord. Nothing.

Naomi had stopped writhing. She looked pale and weak.

I had to do something. I took a huge gulp of air and plunged my head into the water. I pressed my open mouth against hers and blew the air in. Her eyes opened wide in surprise.

My mind flipped through options furiously as I prepared to give her another breath of air. V flashed two options: a laser to cut the cords, or some lever to rip them off.

I plunged my head again and gave Naomi another mouthful. I raised my head and scanned the surroundings. A metal bar was lying underwater, a few feet from Naomi. I didn't even think of why it would be there. I rushed and grabbed it.

I propped the bar under the cord holding Naomi's shoulders down. I fixed the middle of the bar against the concrete edge of the pool. I stepped out of the water and leapt into the air. I slammed my feet down as hard as I could against the end of the bar.

SNAP. The cord ripped free.

Naomi's head surged out of the water. The look on her face was confusing—some blend of fear, relief, gratefulness, and intrigue.

"You weren't supposed to do that," she panted.

"Do what?" I asked. "Save your life?"

She nodded. "You weren't supposed to let anything stop you. It was a test."

I stared deep into her green eyes. "I'm not playing any games that put you at risk."

"Then you'll fail," said Wade's voice from behind me. "You have a lot to learn."

I turned and saw the drone hovering before my eyes. I met its lifeless gaze and spoke with defiance, "I would do the same thing again."

"We'll see," said Wade's voice. "Come on, both of you, grab hold. We're going back to the Pentagon."

Naomi stepped out of the pool to my side.

"What happened to the other cord?" I asked. "The one that bound your legs?"

She shrugged. "I had controls to release it. It was a ploy to divert you."

"The other cord, too, the one on your chest?"

"No." The fear was back in her eyes. "That was a surprise. It sprang out of the pool's bottom and tied me down."

"Wow." Would they really put her life at risk for some test? I shuddered at the thought. "Let's try to stick together," I said.

"Okay," she smiled. "Thank you."

"That's enough," Wade demanded. "We're going to be late, and the Captain hates that. Grab on."

Naomi and I took hold of the loops under the drone.

Our bodies could not help but touch as we soared into the air. I didn't try to pull away, and neither did she. We flew together over the Potomac River, to the Pentagon.

"Orders, orders, orders. Anyone care to guess why ISA-7 agents *must* obey their orders?" The Captain was pacing in front of us. He'd been lecturing our group for an hour about the morning's exercise—with me as his pincushion. We were in the same room as yesterday. At least this time they hadn't tied us to our chairs.

"Agents lack complete information," Patrick volunteered, "so they must do their part for the team."

"That's true," said the Captain, "but it must be understood in context. What is our context?"

"Secrecy," answered Aisha.

The Captain nodded. "And?"

"And protecting the world," added Charles.

The Captain studied Charles. "What are we protecting the world from?"

"Attacks of all kinds, I guess," Charles said. "We spy on

every threat to mankind, so that means we monitor political leaders, terrorists, and hackers with potential to bring destruction."

The Captain began pacing again as he spoke. "That is a fair description of the ISA, but we are more than that. ISA-7 operates within the ISA shroud, protecting the world from the most hidden and serious threats. We watch every nation. We watch every world leader. We even watch our other ISA agents. The best spies make sure regular spies do their job. Why do you think you'll be spending the rest of the day going through ISA orientation in that classroom with Wade?"

"You want us to pretend to be normal ISA student fellows," Naomi answered. "ISA recruits agents with our qualifications from a young age. We'll go back to our schools and no one will expect us to take any missions from there. It's a good cover."

The Captain had stopped pacing and locked eyes with Naomi. "At least someone in this room knows what's going on. Naomi's right. If you meet our standards, we can't afford to hold you back from the field. But if you don't, you're better off leaving now. Anyone?"

His gaze swung to me, boring into me with his blue eyes. The room fell quiet. I met his stare and stayed calm, while my insides turned in circles. If this guy thought he was going to scare me away now, he was wrong. I wouldn't give him the satisfaction of backing down, especially not with Naomi and the others watching.

"Good," the Captain said as he finally looked away

from me. I considered it a battle won. "All of you will need that commitment in the days ahead. If you do not obey your orders, you will fail. And if you fail in the field, the mission of ISA-7 will be compromised. No one can know what we do. The safety of the world depends on it." He paused and looked past our group. "Wade?"

"Yes, Captain," said Wade. This time it was actually him, not a drone. "I'll take them back. We finish HR this morning and will spend the afternoon with an overview of international politics."

"Very well." The Captain saluted and bowed slightly to us. "Remember, there is no greater service than ISA-7. You have much to learn in the exercises to come. Obey your orders and together we will protect the world from itself. See you tonight."

After the Captain left, Wade escorted us towards the classroom. We traced our steps on the underground path we'd taken from the training center to the Pentagon the day before. Each of us stayed quiet and focused, ready for whatever they'd throw at us this time. But nothing happened.

Along the way I began to notice the cameras. They were tiny dots on the ceiling and the walls, like specks of dirt. Once we entered the training building, Charles and I started pointing out a few flies buzzing around. There were enough to be suspicious. They were probably drones with cameras installed. Nothing like the feeling of constantly being watched to make you walk straighter.

We were the first to arrive in the ISA classroom, but

the others joined us soon afterwards. The rest of the day was a boring blur of orientation talks, followed by an evening of lectures from the Captain about ISA-7. No more action, no more tests, but I was exhausted all the same when they finally let us go after midnight. I tried two different dream pills back in my hotel room and fell asleep. It was a dreamless night. Maybe the pills worked this time, or maybe I was too tired to dream.

The next morning came early. We were back in the classroom. Wade was explaining a bunch of org charts and acronyms. The UN liaison glared over the room with a scowl. Occasionally he'd jot down notes. His beady eyes caught mine more than a few times. It made me feel like a kid with his hand in the cookie jar. Or maybe it was just an awkward coincidence. The liaison was probably bored, too. *Question everyone*, the Captain had warned. Right. So maybe the liaison was planning to kill me. I was ISA-7 after all, sneaking off to learn how to monitor anything and anyone, even the UN. Nah, I was just bored.

When classes finally ended, I hurried back to my hotel room and changed. I threw on the most casual outfit I had—jeans and a button-down shirt. It was closer to Naomi's style than my designer suits. My hair was a curly mess, but there was never any helping that.

I made it to the bench five minutes before 8. Naomi was already waiting for me, as graceful as the swooning willow beside her.

"Ready?" she asked.

I smiled. "Promise it'll be more exciting than today?"

"Oh yeah. Probably too exciting."

"Perfect. Lead on."

We walked to the line of auto-taxis by the edge of the park. We crammed into one the size of an overgrown pea.

"Washington National Cathedral," she said. The taxi blinked on a green light and zoomed off.

"The Cathedral?" I asked. I'd never been there before. I'd never wanted to.

"There's a service, and I want to introduce you to some friends."

"I thought this was a date." She had to drag me to something religious already? "I'm not sure this is a good idea."

"Why not?" Her eyes studied mine. Sitting so close, I could feel her breath. It smelled fresh, like strawberry mint.

"You know I'm Jewish," I said.

She nodded. "That makes it easier. We believe in the same God. Jehovah."

"Well...I guess, but," I began to question her logic just as the Cathedral came into view. I figured it was better not to say more if I could avoid it. This was one area where we'd have to agree to disagree. The taxi raced up to the curb, Naomi held her wrist to the scanner to pay, and then we climbed out.

"Come on," she said, "we're late."

I followed her along a stone path towards the Cathedral. Its gothic spires and arches shone against the night sky. The spotlights made the massive building look like a fortress on a hill. There was so much stone, and so little glass, like a place for hiding what's inside. No wonder they didn't build like this anymore. We entered through the ancient wooden doors at the front.

The inside was like an ornate cavern. Giant columns framed a stretch of long, empty pews. There were no more than a handful of sporadically seated people. It would have been serene if not for the dozen or so live screens. They showed an overweight preacher I'd seen on the news before.

"God loves everyone!" the preacher's voice boomed across the vacant space. "He doesn't care what you believe, as long as you believe in him and tolerate everyone." The smile on the man's face looked permanent, as did the sheen of sweat. He droned on about more religious stuff.

I tried to ignore his echoing speech as Naomi led us down the center aisle. She stopped at the end.

"Notice anything missing?" she asked, pointing up and toward the back of the cathedral.

"A screen?" I guessed. "They're everywhere else in here."

"You're funny. No, not screens. How about a cross?" She fingered the one dangling from her necklace. "Churches used to have crosses, you know. These days, to keep government funds flowing, they remove the crosses. Everyone agrees the cross has become a symbol of intolerance."

"Seems right," I said. "How's a cross supposed to make someone like me feel?"

"Well, you're putting up with me so far. Let's see what

else." She grabbed my hand and turned down a side aisle with a bounce in her step.

For the first time, I questioned my decision to come along without asking her more. I never signed up for a conversion experience. I was a bad candidate anyway. The faith of my childhood died an early death, right when my mom did. Still, curiosity kept my feet moving as Naomi tugged me along.

At the side of the cathedral, near the back, we came to stairs leading down. After a couple flights my precept lost its network connection. Great—because things went so well last time that happened. We eventually arrived at a long hallway that felt like a tomb. Halfway down the hall, Naomi knocked on a simple, brown door. After three knocks on the other side, Naomi responded with another quick series of knocks, seven, I thought.

The door opened to a warmly-lit room stuffed with books and people. It looked like an office with the desk shoved up against the far wall, under a cross.

A sharply dressed middle-aged man was leaning back against the desk and holding a book, probably a Bible. About twenty people sat close together on the rug-covered stone floor. They looked nice enough, but the whole thing gave me the chills. It was like one of those dreams where you show up somewhere naked, only this time I had clothes on and the pretty girl had led me to some cult's meeting.

It was not a good start to our date.

9

"Naomi, you made it just in time!" welcomed the sharp-looking man, as everyone in the room turned to stare at us. "We were wrapping up, but it wouldn't have been right to finish without one of your songs. Who's your friend?"

"This is Elijah," Naomi said. Her soft tone gave me more comfort than I cared to admit. "He is one of the other ISA student fellows."

"Impressive." The man suddenly looked wary as he sized me up. "Is he one of us?"

Naomi shook her head. "Not yet," her voice lowered, "but he has *seen* things to come." The way she said that made me shiver. "I want him to talk to Bartholomew."

"And Elijah went up by a whirlwind into heaven." The rumbling voice came from a large man sitting nearby. He wore a brown robe and a long gray goatee. The excitement filling his broad features and pale eyes pushed me a step back, against the door. "I've been waiting a long time for you to come," he said.

"Elijah, don't mind Bart," interrupted the man who had welcomed us. His face tugged at my memory. I felt sure I'd seen him on the news or something. "You must have had some dreams," he said. "Bart can help you with that. But please, come, sit with us. We have just a few minutes left. If you haven't heard Naomi sing, you're in for a treat. Oh, and if you don't mind, could you shut down your precept?"

Shutdown? That was going too far. I looked to Naomi. She smiled at me, a perfect smile. It had to be perfect to keep me from running out of the room—that, plus the chance to hear to her sing again.

"Please?" she asked. "We're safe in here." She gently pulled on my arm to sit beside her near the closed door. She wouldn't lie to my face, would she?

I sighed. "Fine, V, shut down." And then she was gone, leaving my mind bland. It always made me feel alone, even now, sitting in a room of people, with Naomi at my side. None of them could be as close as V.

"Thank you," Naomi said. "We just don't like these meetings recorded."

I nodded, but that wasn't much comfort. What about it didn't they want to record? Still, my breathing calmed slightly as we leaned back against the wall and the room's attention turned again to the leader.

"As I was asking," he said, "based on what we've studied tonight." He held up the book again. Now I felt sure it was a Bible. "Who is our neighbor? Is it the person who lives beside us or is it everyone in the world?"

A tall man in the front stood and turned to the room. He looked very familiar.

"That's my dad," Naomi whispered in my ear. My eyes opened wide. Great, so I could meet her pastor and her father at the same time. What had this girl dragged me into?

His skin was darker than Naomi's, but they had the same athletic poise, the same wide-set eyes. Their faces had a leanness that made it look like they were always running with a breeze on their face.

"As with most things," her dad was saying, "our Lord shows the way." He smiled wide, like Naomi. "So our neighbor is anyone in our path in need." He was looking at me. I tried to stay calm but I felt sweat beading on my face.

"I could not have said it better," the leader responded. "Let me finish with a prayer, then Naomi will lead us in a song and we'll go."

He closed his eyes and bowed his head and began to speak. Everyone else in the room did the same...everyone but me. It was the perfect chance to figure out who these people were. The group ranged in age from teens to grandparents, and their clothes marked some as professionals and a few as homeless, or close to it. Religious meetings like this were against the law because they could not be monitored. No wonder they'd made me shut down V, but I could still report this. At least that gave me some leverage if things went bad.

Suddenly the group all started to speak together. "*Our*

father who art in heaven," they began. I thought I'd heard the words before. Their voices were solemn as they spoke on. It brought back an old memory of a rabbi's voice. *"Amen."* They finally finished together and opened their eyes.

"Naomi?" the leader said.

She stood and stepped carefully through the seated people to the front of the room. She turned to face us. "I think tonight we should end with Be Thou My Vision. Okay?"

The group murmured approval. She cleared her throat lightly and began, *"Be thou my vision..."*

Her voice had even more power in person. As the verses rolled on, I didn't care what words she sang, or what cult she followed. I just wanted to hear her sing. Her pitch rose and fell in beautiful arcs as her face and shoulders and chest breathed in and out. She locked her eyes on mine, and I drank deep of her smile. Eventually her song came to an end and the room fell quiet.

"That's it everyone," the leader announced. "See you all next week. God bless."

The room began to stir and the murmur of conversation grew.

"Elijah, your presence is a gift," said the large man beside me. He put his hand on my shoulder, breaking me out of the spell from Naomi's song. "I would love to hear more of your dreams. Will you come to my office now?" His eager eyes searched mine.

"Well," I began, trying to find the right way to say no.

"Bart, this is Elijah." Naomi had rushed back to us.

"Elijah, this is Bart. I would very much like for you two to talk. I will come, too. Please, Elijah?" She looked at me with a look that was hard to turn down.

"Okay," I said. I'd already come this far. I might as well hear what this guy had to say about my dreams.

"I'm Moses." Naomi's father appeared beside me, holding out his hand. I reached out and shook it. His hand was at least twice the size of mine, and twice as strong.

I'd seen him in V's report on Naomi, but it was different meeting in person. I couldn't believe I was standing in front of the man. He had shocked the sports world when he retired from basketball after only five years as a pro. He'd been one of my childhood heroes at Madison Square Garden.

"Moses Parish?" I asked. "*The* Moses Parish?"

"That's me." He shrugged his giant shoulders. "I played hoops a few years before getting on with God's work. The missionary field is my true calling. If what Naomi says is right, maybe you'll learn your true calling soon enough. Where are you from?"

"New Yor—" I began but Naomi interrupted.

"Daddy, Elijah is here to talk to Bart about a dream. We don't want to overwhelm him."

The tall man smiled at her and nodded. Then he turned to Bart. "You take it easy on him. Not everyone is as eager to talk about dreams as you are."

"Oh, I will," Bart said. "If he's who I think, we'll have plenty to discuss. Things the whole world should know."

"Well, don't jump to any conclusions." Moses turned to

me. "Nice to meet you, Elijah. Hope to see you around here again."

"You too," I replied, still in awe. For once, I would've been glad to talk to a girl's dad a little longer.

But Naomi whisked me away after Bart.

10

Naomi and I followed Bart down the hall. He had a huge ring of keys clanking at his hip. He moved with a forceful sense of purpose.

Maybe Naomi was doing all this just to test whether I trusted her. Maybe she was taking lessons from the Captain. Or maybe she was as honest and pure as she looked, wanting to help me with the dreams.

"Here we are," Bart announced, stopping before a door near the end of the hall. He grabbed his ring of keys and flipped through them until he found one that looked medieval. He unlocked the door and walked in.

It was a tiny office. Two chairs were crammed in front of a desk covered in books with yellowed pages and a chalk-white human skull. The walls were made of the same stone as the outside of the Cathedral. Weirdest of all were the candles. At least a dozen of them flickered and gave off a pale light. I realized there were no lights on the ceiling. There were no signs of electricity. I felt like I was in a castle dungeon.

"Bart is a member of an ancient order," Naomi said. She must have seen the fear or confusion or whatever else was on my face.

"You sure we can't head out for some ice cream?" I asked, half joking. There was only so far I'd go for a girl I'd known three days, even a beautiful one.

"Maybe later," she teased, "but I promise you'll be interested in what Bart has to say. He studies old ways, visions and dreams. He can help you."

"Where were you born, Elijah?" Bart had taken his seat. He was leaning forward with a hungry look in his eyes.

"New York, Upper East Side."

"Where was your father born?"

"Jerusalem. Why does that matter?"

"What is your mother's maiden name?"

"Why do you want to know?" I asked. "You haven't even told me what's going on here. For all I know this is another ISA test and you're trying to crack into my precept."

"Your precept is off, and do I look like a hacker?" Bart asked, dead serious. He looked nothing like a hacker, or even like someone who owned a phone. He sat back in his chair and folded his hands over his belly. "I'm the exception, Elijah. I'm the resistance, the stodgy man who refuses a precept. Please, sit, both of you."

Naomi and I sat in the chairs opposite Bart.

"So you've had disturbing dreams?" he asked.

"Haven't we all?" I countered.

He shook his head. "If Naomi brought you here, your dreams are not like others' dreams."

"That's true," Naomi agreed, turning to me, "but I have not shared a word of what you dreamed. They are yours to reveal or not. I just told Bart that your dreams would be of great interest, and he asked to see you. You can trust him, I promise. If you doubt me, just take a moment to study what's around us." She motioned to our surroundings and laughed softly. "There's not an ounce of technology from the past hundred years. The ISA couldn't stand a place like this."

She was right. From the looks of things, this old man still read by candlelight. "What's with the skull?" I asked.

"Saint Jerome." Bart looked at me expectantly and probably saw a blank stare on my face. "You don't know Saint Jerome?"

I shook my head.

"He's a saint of my order. He kept a skull, too. *Memonto mori*, it is said. Remember that you will die."

"I'd rather not," I said. "I'm alive now, and that's enough for me. Better to live than to worry about dying."

"Ah, but to remember is not to worry. Death brings no fear for me. Your dreams, however, those might make me fear." He paused, light blue eyes locked on my face. "Please, tell me about them."

I looked at Naomi. She nodded encouragingly. I saw little harm in it, and maybe I was kind of starting to feel curious about what this strange man would say. So I recounted my dreams as I had with Naomi—the dragon and all that I'd seen in Rome.

Bart took notes with a pen while I talked. Another person writing on paper—what a weird week. Bart did not interrupt me, but his face took on intrigued expressions at certain points. When I described the man who walked towards the dragon, Bart looked as if his archenemy was walking towards him with a gun. By the end, Bart had filled half a page with notes and cryptic drawings.

"Thank you." He stopped scribbling. "Anything else?"

"No," I answered, "thankfully I found some dream pills that seem to work."

"No more of those!" he snapped. "Your dreams are priceless, and indeed essential. Give me your word."

"What? That I won't take some pills?"

He nodded.

I didn't feel like having more nightmares, but the pills weren't a sure thing anyway. "I'll hold off on them for a while."

"I guess that'll do," he sighed. "Now, I'd like to ask you some questions." He sounded eager to dissect me.

"Fine, but I'm not promising any answers. They're just dreams."

"Just dreams," Bart smiled, "until they become real." He put down his pen and leaned forward with his elbows on the desk. "You said there were storms. Was it warm outside?"

"I don't know."

"Think hard."

"I don't remember."

"Were you wearing a jacket?"

"A jacket?"

He nodded.

"Yeah, a tweed sports coat."

"Were there flowers?"

"I don't know, maybe. What's the point?"

"*When?*" he drawled out. "I'm trying to figure out when this happened."

"It didn't *happen*. It was a dream."

"You said the city was crowded. Was the piazza full?"

"There were a lot of people. More than I could count."

Naomi spoke next, "It could be Holy W—"

Bart held up his pudgy hand to stop her. I noticed for the first time a thick ring on his thumb, made of some skin-colored composite.

"No one knows the time," Bart said, but his excited smile made me think he knew more than he was saying. "Next time you have the dream, you will come to me that very day."

"We'll see," I said. "Do you think it means something?"

"I do, but you don't."

"So tell me what you think."

"Not tonight." His tone allowed no debate. "I will tell you more after the next one."

"What makes you think I'll have the dream again?"

"You will, because it is meant to be." His answer was as certain as the skull on his desk was dead.

"So what if I do? What makes you think I'll come back?"

"You want to know more, and I can give you answers. Plus—" he glanced at Naomi, and then at me again—"how many boys do you think have tried to court her?"

I flushed.

"You're clever, Elijah, but I've been around a lot longer than you have. She wants you to come next time you have the dream, right Naomi?"

She nodded, smiling.

I tried not to notice how good she looked in the candlelight. "We'll see," I said. "I don't think I'll have the dream again."

"What's your mother's maiden name?" Bart repeated his earlier question.

"None of your business," I replied. My mom had been dead ten years, and the last thing I wanted to do was talk about her with this man.

"My business is helping you, so that you can do your business. What's her maiden name?" he demanded.

"Roeh. You happy now?"

Bart shook his head no. "Now I'm scared. You will have another dream, only next time it will be worse."

"Worse?"

"Yes, and then you'll start to believe. You two will come to me, and we will talk more."

Despite my attempts at denial, Bart was right. The dream came again that night.

11

The creature's red eyes locked on me. Just like last time, I was on the ground looking out over St. Peter's Basilica in crumbles and the piazza in chaos. The man was standing beside the dragon. He was the finest looking man I had ever seen. His clothes were modern and trim. His face was cut from an advertisement. It was a face I knew.

Suddenly the creature turned from me to the man, making me feel like a heavy blackness had lifted. The creature spoke. It was almost like words, but not in any language I had heard. The man nodded as if he understood. Then he walked towards me.

I wanted to move, but I could not. The red eyes were on me again. The heavy blackness was on me again.

"Elijah." It was Naomi's voice. She was beside me.

"Elijah," she repeated. "He is coming at us."

It took every ounce of will to turn to her. She was

sitting on the ground with her legs crossed, hugging herself. Her face and body strained forward, as if a thousand invisible cords tied her down.

"We can't move," I said.

"I know. He's here."

"*Naomi.*" The man was standing over us. He was tall and thin. The only wide thing about him was his smile. It stretched across his face in sheer delight.

"No!" Naomi shouted, straining against whatever held her down.

"Naomi, dear Naomi, you know better than to speak to me." He was waving his finger in disapproval. "Quiet now," he ordered.

Her lips sealed tight. The look on her eyes was one of both sheer terror and defeat.

"Elijah, I'm afraid we have not met." The man's voice was smooth and welcoming. He held out his hand to me. "I'm Abaddon, but call me Don."

His gentle words thawed my frozen muscles so that I could move. I flexed my hand and my arm. I began to reach up to shake his hand.

"*NO!*" Naomi's scream shattered the vision like a rock through glass.

I awoke covered in sweat. Not a good start to my Thursday.

I tried not to think of the dream as I went through my morning routine. I tried not to think of it as I walked to breakfast. I tried not to think of it as I greeted Charles and Patrick. But the dream was still there, boiling under the surface of my subconscious, its vapors drifting up, swirling with Bart's warning, and clouding my thoughts.

"So, only two days left in our first week," Patrick said as he chomped his eggs, "and seems like you and Naomi are already a thing." He was studying me.

"I don't know about that," I replied. I could still hear her terrified scream in my mind. "It's complicated. We're not exactly each other's type, you know." I hid behind a long drink of milk.

"Oh I think she's your type," Charles chimed in, "with those long legs and wholesome round…eyes, you know."

"Enough," I said, failing to suppress a tiny smile.

"Hey, I just tell it like it is." Charles held up his hands in innocence. "But I think Patrick's right. No matter how many guys have wanted her, I bet she hasn't had one like you coming after her. Within a day, you were making out with her in the reflecting pool."

"You know that's not true. I was giving her oxygen."

"Yeah, mouth-to-mouth oxygen during an ISA drill. Not bad, Eli. It must have worked, because you had her begging you to come with her on a date. Where did you go last night, anyway?"

"Good question," Patrick added. "A romantic stroll along the Potomac?"

I laughed. "That would've been nice."

"Special training for our test on Friday?" Charles asked.

"Something like that," I said. "And what about you Charles? How are things coming with Aisha?"

"I've got her right where I want her," he answered.

"Turns out Patrick here is a savvy third wheel. Last night, while you and Naomi were somewhere making out, he and I went with Aisha to a show at the Kennedy Center. We had two extra tickets since you and Naomi bailed on us. Patrick invited the pretty twins from the bigger ISA class." He looked to Patrick. "What were their names?"

"Mary and Sarah," Patrick answered.

"Classy names," I said. "Were they born in the last century?"

"They are barely older than we are. They go to Georgetown," Patrick bragged, probably proud to have gone out with college girls. "Never met anyone named Mary in Manhattan?"

"A few grandmothers," I said. "I know one who might like you."

"Oh, is she too tall for you?" Patrick taunted.

"C'mon guys," Charles interrupted. "As I was saying, the five of us went to the show. After it was over, Patrick ducked away with his two guests and, yes Elijah, they were cute. We can't *all* have Naomi. But the important thing is, Patrick being the good guy he is, he left Aisha and me alone. Guess who got to first base?"

"You held her hand?" Patrick asked.

Charles and I burst out into laughter. Then I realized from Patrick's confused stare that he wasn't joking.

"Are things really that different in Catholic school?" I asked.

"What do you mean?" he replied.

"First base is holding hands?"

"Yeah, what is it for you?"

"Primary level data syncing," Charles answered, pointing to his temple where the main precept chip was installed. "You know, exchanging all your media files and bio-data. When you know a girl's heart rate every moment, then you're on your way to second base."

"Wow," Patrick's mouth hung open. "That's definitely past second base for us." He turned to me. "You didn't sync with Naomi already, did you?"

"I bet he did." Charles looked at me eagerly.

"No." I stared down at my empty plate. Then I remembered how close Naomi was to me in the dream. It felt like we were already connected. I had shared my dream with her, and she had exposed her secret order. We were both vulnerable, but she was still hiding something. I felt sure of it.

I looked up and held Charles and Patrick's attention. "Not yet, anyway." I forced myself to grin, and to say what they probably expected me to say. "I will sync with her before this week's over. You can count on it."

12

I flew straight at the Shanghai skyscraper.

When I reached its wall of glass, I dove down, plummeting with the city's hot air rushing past me. I stopped and hovered twenty feet above the ground.

People hurried about below me. None of them glanced up. It looked like lunch hour.

How are we supposed to find the target in this chaos? I asked in my mind.

Over here, Aisha answered my thought. *I think this is him.*

I summoned her screen. She was only a hundred feet away, by the edge of the river. A well-dressed man walked in front of her. He carried a black briefcase that looked the right size.

Should we all come? The question came from Charles. He was halfway across the city in front of some meat market.

Come closer and be ready. Aisha's thought sprang into my

mind. *Patrick, head this man off. Elijah, right flank. Naomi, left flank.*

I soared up another twenty feet and flew around the nearest building to monitor the right flank. While I waited for the man to approach, I checked Naomi's screen. She was hovering over the middle of the river. I could smell her air. It was fresh, and so were her thoughts. All the data from her system was more real, as if I was experiencing it exactly as she did.

Look, Naomi suddenly warned, *behind you!*

It was too late. A shock rolled through my body and mind, and I was ejected.

My senses came to the present, to the simulation room. I removed my headset and its link to V. My four teammates were still immersed, as were our five opponents sitting on the opposite side of the room.

I stood and watched ten screens on the far wall. Nine of them were active, showing exactly what the nine remaining players saw. The screen showing my device was frozen. The melon-sized drone I had controlled was on the ground, motionless. It looked like a messenger drone with robotic frog legs. But when I was connected to it, the machine felt like an extension of me. They used to say worlds like this were virtual. Now they were real, because where the mind goes, reality follows.

"That's what happens when you let emotions distract you." The Captain's disappointed voice filled the room.

"I didn't let emotions distract me," I defended.

"You checked your teammate's status." He stepped to

my side and pointed to my screen. "Look at 4:43:27." The image rolled back to that moment. "Your instinct was right," he said. "The right flank must check the left flank. So far so good. But here, at 4:43:35, you are lingering on Naomi's status. You already knew what you needed—her position, her line of sight. You did not need to stay to know what she smelled. She tried to save you, but you were already lost. Agent 8 had been tracking you. He saw your drone holding still as seconds ticked away. He took you out before you even saw him coming."

"I'll do better next time," I said.

"You are lucky to get another try," the Captain warned. "You are lucky to be here at all. Your father owes me one. Now shape up, boy. You fail the test tomorrow, and you're out of luck." He turned away and studied the screens.

A moment later Patrick and two of the opponents were ejected from the simulation.

"We took them out!" Patrick gasped, as if bursting out of water for air.

"And you died," the Captain said. "You took an unnecessary risk. Watch and learn."

The Captain walked over to a chair where an opponent was sitting, just ejected from the simulation. The man rose at the Captain's command. The Captain sat and lifted the headset.

"But you said it was a simple five-on-five," Patrick protested.

"And I told you to trust no one," the Captain said. "The enemy will not follow the rules. Neither do I. Watch."

He lowered the headset and his eyes closed. His face became intensely concentrated.

I turned to the screen showing what the Captain saw. He soared at a faster pace than the rest of us. He swept high in the air and then dove straight down, his view zooming onto the man with the briefcase.

The man ducked into a building and Aisha's drone followed him in. My eyes jumped from screen to screen, to watch the action unfold. Charles and Naomi took up guard outside. Their screens showed them scanning all around.

The Captain launched a shot from an impossible distance. The missile looked like a tiny, soaring bird until the instant it opened into a net. The net snared Naomi's drone and sent it shaking and falling to the ground.

"Hey!" Naomi shouted as her consciousness returned to the room. "We knew where the agents were. Someone must have taken over an agent who was down."

As she stood, she glanced in the direction of the Captain. His eyes were still closed. Her face darkened knowingly. We exchanged a quick glance, and then turned to study the screens.

Charles's machine had moved inside the building. It was a noodle shop. A few patrons eyed the floating drones warily. The man with the briefcase was at the counter. Our mission was to get the briefcase and leave the man untouched. Charles flew up beside his right ear. The drone was about the size of the man's head.

The man turned to Charles. Then Aisha's drone dashed out from the other side of the counter and its claw snatched the briefcase.

Another drone appeared in the room and fired at Charles just as Aisha fired at it. The opponent and Charles both went down, and Aisha's drone burst out a window with the briefcase.

She flew free for only a moment before her view of the smog-ridden sky jarred, blinked, and went black.

The Captain's screen showed Aisha's machine bound in a net and crashing to the ground.

13

"Failure." The Captain's voice was in the room again. He was pulling off his headset. "What did you do wrong?"

"We were too aggressive," Aisha said, as she and Charles joined the rest of us.

"Correct," the Captain answered. "We are not the military. We do not bash into restaurants and pick fights. We watch and we wait. We wait and we watch. Only when the perfect moment comes do we act. We cannot risk discovery."

"But we would have won," Patrick said, "if you hadn't cheated."

"Cheated? What rule did I break?" The Captain stepped up to Patrick. The older man was a head shorter, but looked like a predator. "There are no rules in this game, boy. If you want rules, join the armed forces. Here you're not going to get orders in the field. All you're going to have is your wits and your teammates." The man's bald head leaned closer to Patrick's face. "You think it was a good trade? You go down and take two with you?"

"Yes, absolutely," Patrick began, but then he shrank back under the Captain's stare. "Well, I guess it depends."

"There are no good trades for ISA-7," the Captain said. "Why not, Wade?"

Our instructor had joined the room without me noticing. He walked up to the Captain's side and smiled at us. "You are the world's frontline for intelligence and thus peace," he said. "We pour immense resources into training you and equipping you. The drones you'll ultimately be operating cost as much as this whole simulation room. No one outside of ISA-7 knows they exist. We must keep them hidden behind ISA's public face. If you get an opportunity to sacrifice yourself to save a million lives, then we'll think about the trade. Otherwise, the Captain is right—you never reveal yourself while on mission."

"Your entrance examination is tomorrow," the Captain said. "I expect better from each of you." His gaze settled on me. "Fail tomorrow, and say goodbye to ISA-7. Better yet, if you harbor a single doubt, don't show up again. A few of you might have what it takes. We'll see."

The Captain walked out. No salute this time.

"Sven?" Wade looked to the skinny guy who had been the last one left in the simulation with the Captain. "Time to tell them more about the drones."

"Sooo, want to learn about drones?" asked Sven. He looked like an under-slept Nordic hacker who was barely older than we were. He had blood-shot eyes, thick dark glasses, and wild blonde hair. "Wasn't that exercise amazing?" He was practically bouncing on the floor, either from excitement or from way too much caffeine.

"It was cool," Charles answered. "A little better than some of the games I've played. Your recreation of Shanghai was impressive. It felt very real."

A smile stretched over Sven's face. "That *was* real! We didn't make up anything about Shanghai, other than instructing the target about the exercise."

"Seriously?" Patrick looked as surprised as I felt. No one had mentioned the simulation would be in the real world.

"Seriously." Sven was still bouncing from foot to foot. "Why do you think we made your drones look like standard package deliverers? Those little helicopters are everywhere in Shanghai these days, and so are minor drone attacks. It's standard corporate espionage." He took a deep breath. "Just wait until you try our best drones."

"What are they?" Charles sounded eager. "Fighter planes, tiny machines the size of bugs?"

Sven shook his head. "Are their precepts secure?" he asked Wade. "Is it time?"

Wade nodded. "They're clean. Fire away."

"You'll be operating human bodies," Sven said.

"Live bodies?" Naomi's eyes opened wide.

"No way, not alive!" Sven answered. "We can't control others' minds, not yet at least. But we can reconstruct a fresh corpse, preserve its flesh a while, and rebuild its nerve system with circuits. Then you can occupy it completely when we link your precept. This sync is more comprehensive than with the messenger drones, and it is much more dangerous."

"When do we try it?" Charles seemed more excited than the rest of us combined. Maybe this was going too far. Sure, we could grow organs and control prosthetics with our minds, but corpses?

"Someday soon," Sven said, "but first you'll have to prove your sync capacity is high enough, and we'll have to upgrade your precepts. If you pass the exam tomorrow and enlist fully in ISA-7, we'll do those things right away." He held his arms wide like the ringmaster of a techno-circus. "Human existence is changing, my friends."

"Bet y'all will never look at another person the same way, will ya?" Wade asked.

"How long has this been going on?" Naomi glared at Sven and Wade. Her voice and presence made them look small.

"We passed the first prototype only a few years ago," Sven explained, ignoring Naomi's tone. "The Captain was the first one to survive the process."

"How many died?" Patrick asked, looking a little pale.

"Why did they die?" I added.

"We lost more than we care to admit," Sven said. "And we don't know exactly why. Something strange happens when you sync completely with another human body. We're still trying to figure it out."

"Don't worry," Wade chimed in. "Every agent who has

passed tomorrow's test and handled the precept upgrade has been fine. We're not losing any of you to failed syncs." He held up three fingers pressed together. "Scout's honor!"

"Friends, you're in good hands with Wade." Sven clapped his hand on Wade's shoulder. "He got me through this process a few years ago. Listen to him. He's more than meets the eye."

"And here I thought I was just easy on the eyes." Wade winked with a weak attempt at charm. "See ya, Sven."

"Bye everyone!" Sven bowed to us. "We'll be talking lots in the days to come. Good luck tomorrow."

Sven left and Wade began telling us the schedule for the rest of the day. My thoughts ran ahead to tomorrow's test. I had assumed we would all pass, with the scores mattering only for assignments and rank. Surely I would pass. They did not bring me here to push UN bureaucracy with the rest of the ISA. As creepy as it sounded, I wanted to try operating another body. No wonder ISA-7 kept everything so secret.

"So to wrap up," Wade was saying, "lunch break now, then we're in the classroom for a couple hours and back here for the rest of the afternoon. See you at 1 pm sharp."

14

"You were good in there," Naomi said, as we made our way to lunch. Charles, Aisha, and Patrick had walked on ahead of us.

"If I was good, I wouldn't have been the first out." The Captain's criticism still had me shaken up.

"I saw your metrics," Naomi encouraged.

"And?"

"Your syncing was in the top three."

I tried to hide my surprise. "Was the Captain first?"

Naomi nodded.

"What was my rate?" I asked.

"95%."

My breath caught. Earlier Wade had said most trainees synced their minds and precepts with a drone's movements 80% of the time. "What were the rest of us?"

"We were all above 90%." She smiled confidently.

"They picked us for a reason, but we have room to improve. The Captain was at 100%."

That seemed impossible. "What was your rate?"

"Not perfect." Her voice hinted at frustration. She looked away and glanced around the cafeteria. "How about shakes instead of just water and pills today? Hey look, there's Patrick, Charles, and Aisha. Let's join them."

Our three classmates had already gotten their lunches and were sitting outside. "Okay," I smiled at her, "lunch outside with the group. But before we go, tell me your rate, and how you did it, then I'll tell you what I dreamed last night."

"Another dream?" she whispered, studying my face.

"Yes, what was your rate?"

She looked down, a touch of red on her cheeks. "98%."

"What!" I could not believe it. "It takes agents years of training to be that good."

"I want to be better than good." Her gaze returned to me. "You would have been at 98% if not for your last minute."

"What do you mean?"

"Your last minute," she said, "when you checked in on my status. That was when your rate dropped. You had been at 98% sync before then."

"Wow." I'd expected to do well, but that was amazing. "Did the metrics show why my rate dropped so much?"

More color came to her cheeks. "You know how your mind syncs with your drone?"

"Yeah?"

"Well, in the same way, you started to sync *into* my drone, which pulled you away from your own drone. You were at an 87% sync with my drone when you were taken out."

"But doesn't it take special training to partner like that?" I felt heat coming to my own cheeks.

"Usually, that's what I've heard." She let out a slight, uncomfortable laugh. "I'll have to be more cautious when flying with you."

"Or maybe we'll have to make it an official partnership." Maybe "partnership" was ambiguous, and maybe that's because I wanted to see how she'd take it.

But she deflected my idea. "We'll see," she said, motioning to the food distributor. "Let's get our shakes while you tell me about your dream." She started to walk away.

I began to follow after her but my feet froze. A video screen on the far wall showed a man speaking before an assembly. I stepped closer. He was the President of the UN, and I knew his face.

Naomi had stopped and turned back to me. "What's wrong?" she asked.

"The dream," I said under my breath.

"What about it?"

The images crowded my senses. I could see the man standing over Naomi and me. I could hear her screaming, *No!* The memory was clear as day.

"What happened?" She tugged my arm gently and guided me to a corner of the room where no one was nearby. "It's okay, tell me. No one can hear us now."

"I had the dream again. Most of it was the same. But," I swallowed, "but this time you were there. The man, he spoke to us."

"What did he say?"

"He commanded you not to talk."

"What else? Who was he?"

I shook my head. I did not want to admit how the man had spoken to me, like he *knew* me. "He looked like the President of the UN."

"Donatello Cristo?"

"Yeah."

"But he's…" she paused, "he's the most powerful man in the world. Why didn't you say it was him before?"

"I don't know. I thought I recognized him, but it was like there was block in my mind…like he wouldn't *allow* me to know who he was. But when I just saw him on the news over there, it hit me like a ton of bricks."

"So what else did he say?"

"Nothing really," I lied. Then I remembered the way he'd looked at me. I'd never seen a man so…so *appealing*. "Well, one thing," I admitted, "he introduced himself to me. He called himself a weird name—Abaddon. That was it. Then I woke up."

Her face had gone white. She hesitated before speaking but her words came out with quiet certainty. "You must come with me to see Bart again tonight."

"I'd rather not," I said. "Maybe I'm better not knowing his theories."

"Please?" She took my hand in hers and stepped closer.

I glanced down at our hands. Together. Touching. I looked back at her eyes. My resistance crumbled. There was no way I could say no. I tried to rationalize it: Bart could at least be a little amusing, even if he was crazy, so I'd be sure to hear something interesting.

"I will go," I agreed, "but will you let me take you somewhere tomorrow, after the test?"

"Where?"

"Somewhere special, a surprise. We'll come back on Saturday morning."

She let go of my hand. "I'm not sharing a room with you."

"Of course not," I said innocently. "Separate rooms, separate beds, I just want to get away. We'll find some fresh country air."

She eyed me like a fish studying a worm on a hook. "These plans are not of your making, Elijah."

"What's that supposed to mean?"

"Your dreams," she said, "and us. This is all part of something bigger."

"Us?" I smiled. If "us" was part of something bigger, maybe I'd be okay with that. Hadn't I accepted the ISA invitation to join something bigger in the first place? "So, does that mean you're up for a surprise trip?"

She hesitated, her expression guarded. "Separate rooms, and nothing strange, you promise?"

"I promise. Knight's honor."

"Elijah the Knight." She smiled. "Okay, I'll join you for

some fresh country air as long as things go well between now and then." *No pressure!* I thought, as she glanced out the window toward Patrick, Charles, and Aisha. "Come on, I'm hungry," she said, "and those three are going to think we're dating or something."

"Would that be so bad?" I asked.

"Funny! Anyone dating me would know better than to keep me away from lunch." She patted her flat stomach.

"Then what are we waiting for? Shakes await."

And so did another date, if I could survive another encounter with Bart.

15

After Thursday's classes and another simulation, I had an hour—a sweet, unscheduled hour—until I'd meet Naomi. She had roped me into dinner at some famous preacher's house before the meeting with Bart. It seemed like a small price to pay, especially since Naomi would be there in her evening finest.

But now my mind spun around the best ways to spend my free hour. I made my way back to my hotel room and, once inside, instructed V to give her daily report. I had sixty-seven direct messages and nine news briefings. For once, I ignored them. They could wait.

"Research. President of the United Nations," I ordered. "Report on what you find after thirty minutes." The man's face still gnawed at my memory. Perhaps it made sense that my dreams would include a man I'd seen before, but nothing else about the dreams made sense at all.

"Research. ISA entrance examination," I ordered. "Summary report in forty minutes." It still seemed odd that we had to pass the exam. Not that I'd have any trouble passing. Surely I'd get the highest score, except maybe for Naomi. But before, everyone had said it was a placement exam. Now the Captain had changed the story and said we had to pass, and he had mentioned my dad in the same breath. That was troubling, to say the least.

I plopped down into the plush leather chair in the corner of my room. I almost felt comfortable, staring at the ceiling. But my thoughts still spun. Naomi, my dad, tomorrow's test, the UN President, my dreams. Life was simpler a week ago, when I was just a kid about to graduate from high school. I needed a break.

"Where's my dad?" I asked.

"Turks and Caicos," answered V, "on a beach." She sounded awfully cheery. I guess that's why I picked the Australian accent. Maybe I'd change that soon. V might sound nice as a Brit.

"Order me a piña colada and shift me there," I commanded.

"Order placed," V said. "Activating lenses."

I blinked and held my eyes closed for several seconds. When I opened them, turquoise water and an empty white sand beach filled my vision. I could hear the gentle sound of waves. I could feel the breeze on my skin, the sand between my toes. Those nerve-endings were easy to control for the best precept on the market.

An android delivered my drink, complete with a

tropical umbrella. V knew me well. I took a sip and let my mind drift to the tropics. If my dad was relaxing there, so would I.

The minutes passed in quiet, and I drank down the piña colada. I may have dozed off before V woke me with a gentle alarm in my mind. The ocean was gone. There was no more breeze. I didn't have much time before I needed to leave to meet Naomi.

"First report," I said.

"The President of the United Nations," V began. The screen came on before me, showing his face. It was hard to imagine a more perfect face. "Donatello Cristo. Born in Rome in 2022. Unusual—no trace of birth details. Nothing known of his parents. Adopted and raised in a privileged home. Highest test scores of all high school graduates in Italy. EU scholar for university studies in programming. Founded security software company, then went public." The screen streamed a video of him standing over the International Stock Exchange. "He became the youngest-ever European billionaire. Then he attended Oxford for his doctorate in religion. In 2056, at thirty-four years old, Italy designated him for the UN General Assembly. He was elected six years ago to the UN Presidency." The screen flashed to a video that looked like an acceptance speech. "At 38, he was the youngest-ever UN President. He also has the highest approval ratings ever—currently 78%. His numbers soared after UN drones quelled the U.S.-China Cold War and repaired the rifts from the great earthquake of 2063. Re-election is expected this year."

V stopped there. She probably expected me to follow up on one of her points. I did not. Time was too short, or at least that's what I told myself. I tried to ignore the fear growing out of my unanswered questions—why would a man like that show up in my dreams, and why would it seem so real?

"Next report," I said.

"ISA entrance examination. No information found."

"What?" That was absurd. V always found something.

"No information found," she repeated.

I started thinking of other ways to frame the request. Then someone knocked on my hotel room door.

Maybe it was Naomi, coming early to surprise me. Or another piña colada, compliments of the hotel? God knows my dad had spent enough money in this hotel over the years.

I opened the door and a blur swept past me. I spun, closing the door behind me, and saw Aisha.

"Disconnect your precept," she demanded. She was breathing heavily.

"What?"

"Disconnect it."

"Why?"

"I need to tell you something important."

"About what?"

She blinked her lush lashes and glared at me impatiently. "I *said* disconnect it."

"Fine, I will if you will."

"I already did." She tapped her temple. "Scan me."

I ran V's area sweep. Aisha's precept was not showing up.

"Disconnect V and confirm," I ordered.

"Precept disconnected," V responded. "Reboot on command."

Aisha gave me a satisfied look.

"So?" I asked. "This better be fast. I'm meeting Naomi in ten minutes."

"That's why I came," she whispered, stepping closer to me. "You can't trust her."

That didn't make any sense. Aisha and Naomi were friends, weren't they? "What's wrong?" I asked. "Did she do something to you?"

"No, I trust her, but you can't. Her loyalties lie elsewhere." There was desperation in Aisha's voice. She sounded serious.

"Why are you telling me this?" I asked.

She hesitated. "Charles wanted me to."

"Then why wouldn't he tell me?"

"He's on a mission tonight. I can't say more."

"But we haven't finished training or passed the entrance exam."

"I can't say more. Charles said you wouldn't believe me, so he told me to tell you, 'pick tigers at lunch, over tomato soup.'"

Only Charles would know to say that. He and I had talked together about Princeton, the Tigers, over lunch at school one day. We had been eating tomato soup.

"You satisfied?" Aisha asked. She must have seen the

familiar memory pass across my face. I had to work on that.

I was satisfied she had heard something from Charles, but I wasn't going to say as much. "I hear your warning," I said, "and I will think about it."

"Yes, you must." She put her hands on my shoulders and stared up into my eyes. Her eyes were dark pools. "Be careful tonight and good luck on the test."

"Thanks," I smiled, "but I don't think I'll need luck."

She did not smile back. "We all need luck in this game. Luck, God, or both." Then she left, gone as soon as she had come.

"Reboot V," I said.

"Awaiting command."

"Research. Connections between Aisha Mahdi, Charles Chang, and Naomi Parish. Exhaustive report."

I rushed out the door, late for my date.

16

"Maybe someday I'll be a preacher, too." I looked up at the mansion. "A dead president must have lived here. No one builds houses like this anymore."

Naomi laughed. The sound was becoming addictive.

"Preacher?" she asked. "Last I checked, you're Jewish, and you don't need the money."

"Guilty." I pretended to plea with my hands. "But won't they make an exception for me if you ask nicely? I've always wanted to be on the big screen."

"Only the brightest preachers make it that far."

"So what's holding you up?" I asked.

Her face was suddenly serious. "I have a different calling."

"Sorry, didn't know it was a touchy subject." What did she think her *calling* was? I thought of Aisha's warning.

"No worries. It's just that preaching is no joke." She

turned up the mansion's front stairs. "Let's head in, you're going to like Chris and his family."

"Family?" I asked, but she had already stepped onto the guest register.

A beam of light peeked out of the ivy-covered stone wall and scanned our faces. The door swung open a moment later.

"Just an hour, right?" I asked.

She nodded. "But I bet you'll want to come back. You and Chris have more in common than you think."

"We'll see." I doubted it, but surely this guy would be better than Bart.

We walked down an entry hall with parquet floors. Paintings of stoic-looking men in robes lined the walls. The sound of kids yelling and laughing bounded toward us.

"You didn't mention children," I said. "I'm allergic to them."

"I told you we'd be eating with his family."

"I'm an only child. Family means one kid and a nanny."

"How sad!" she said. "Chris and Brie have seven kids."

"Seven. Wow." I'd never seen such a big family in person. They were nearly extinct in the developed world.

The hall's lights suddenly blinked off. I dropped to the floor by instinct. Out of nowhere, I heard a dog's fierce growling just a few feet behind me. I could not see anything. I tensed to defend myself.

"Peter!" a man shouted.

The lights blinked on again. What I thought was a dog was a toe-headed boy, maybe four years old. He was tapping something on his wrist—the source of the growling sound.

"I'm so sorry." A man rushed up and helped Naomi and me to our feet. He was the same man who had been leading the underground study at the Cathedral the night before.

"Welcome!" he said. "I'm Chris, and this is Peter." He pointed to the kid. "He is a bright boy, but his latest game is surprising our guests." He bent down and whispered to his son. "Peter, remember what we said about guests?"

"Sorry Daddy," the boy drawled out. "We have to love them and be nice." His big, round blue eyes fixed on me, then wandered past me. His face lit up. "Naomi!" he shouted as he ran to her.

"Hi Peter!" she greeted, bending down to hug him.

"Let's go, Peter," said a young girl's voice. "We need to finish setting the table." The girl walked past me and scooped up the boy in her arms. She looked eight or nine—I could never tell—but she was dressed like a doll. "I'm Sarah," she said to me. She had the same open innocence as Naomi.

"I'm Elijah. Nice to meet you."

Both the girl and the boy suddenly looked at me with surprise.

"Daddy, is this *the* Elijah?" the boy asked, while the girl whispered "shush" into his ear.

"I don't know yet," the father said. He winked at the boy. "Maybe we'll find out tonight. Run along now. We'll be right behind you."

"It is wonderful to be here," Naomi said, as the girl walked off with the boy. "Thank you so much for having us."

"Of course, it is my pleasure." The man looked to me. "As I was saying, I'm Christopher Max. Please call me Chris. And sorry I didn't get a chance to introduce myself last night."

I shook his hand. "I'm Elijah Goldsmith." Standing this close, I was sure I'd seen his face before last night. "Have I seen you on the news?"

"Yes." He flashed his broadcast smile. "Tonight you can see me without my makeup on. My wife says it's quite the change."

Naomi laughed, but I wasn't sure what was funny. He looked pretty much the same. Perfect brown hair, chiseled face, and bright blue eyes. The only difference I could see was he had taken off his white robe.

"Alright, dinner time," Chris said, turning to lead us down the hall. "I understand you can stay only an hour tonight?"

"Unfortunately," Naomi answered. "We need to visit Bart again."

"Another dream?" Chris asked.

I nodded and opened my mouth to say something dismissive, but the words floated away as we entered the kitchen. It was as luxurious as any I'd seen—sleek counters, rich wooden floors, and all the best technology. That was nothing new for me, but the flurry of action was. Dashing around the room were more kids than I could count. I guessed there were seven, but it looked like seventy. They were running and laughing and playing. At the center of the chaos was one of the most gorgeous women I'd ever seen.

"Welcome to our family nerve center," Chris announced. "This is my wife, Brianne."

She had flaxen blonde hair and a model's face and body. Her white apron was covered in lace and lacked any sign of cooking. It covered a short black dress revealing her long legs and high heels.

"Welcome, and please, call me Brie." she greeted us with a smile that matched Chris's. "I hear one of the twins gave you quite a scare." She embraced Naomi and then turned to me.

"This is Elijah," Chris said from beside us. I held out my hand, but she stepped past it and engulfed me in a hug. She smelled like sweet cinnamon.

"Only hugs in our family," Brie laughed, "and under our roof, you're family. Now, let's have some food!"

The little blond boy, Peter, and a girl about his age caught Brie as we walked through the kitchen.

"Can we come, Mommy?" the girl asked. She had blonde ringlets and her mother's blue eyes.

"This is an adult dinner, my darlings." Brie bent and kissed them, then led us into another hall.

"They're all yours?" I asked. It seemed impossible. She was too young, too attractive. Naomi looked at me as if it were a rude question.

"Sure are," Brie said proudly. "Seven kids under seven! Of course, I didn't give birth to any of them, but we've been blessed with good surrogates."

Chris opened a door before us to an ornate dining room. A table the size of a whale stretched the length of the marble floor. Four places were set with silver and crystal at the nearest end.

"Here we are," Chris said. He turned to me with a grin. "You like scotch?"

"I guess so." I'd never expected a preacher to offer scotch, even if it had been legal for me since last year. Maybe it was his way to show respect, treating me like an adult. My dad would have done the same thing, but my dad was always trying to enthrall people. This guy was starting to remind me of him.

"Good, let's go have a drink. We'll join the ladies for dinner shortly."

Naomi and I shared a look. She nodded for me to go, with the enthusiasm of a mother urging her son to walk into school on his first day. And so I went, with Aisha's words in mind. At least I'd set V's security settings on high.

I was ready for anything, except what came next.

17

Chris led me to a library with books covering every wall but one. Two deep leather chairs sat before a thick oak desk. Behind the desk was a twenty-foot-high wall of glass, framing a view of trees over Rock Creek Park far below. There were no screens to be seen.

"This is my study," Chris said. His casual tone did not match the room's grandeur. "Like my collection?" he asked, as he began to pour scotch into crystal tumblers. "You know, over half of these books have not been digitized. They are rare and priceless works of the faith, entrusted to my keeping."

I reached to pull out a particularly old book nearby. My hand hit an invisible wall, like a forcefield.

"Sorry, no touching." Chris handed me a glass. "These are shielded from anyone and anything that doesn't have my DNA. Being a bishop has its perks."

"Bishop?" I asked. "Isn't that only for Catholics?"

"Not up on your church history, eh?" He effortlessly retrieved the book I had reached for and held it out to me. "For years now, the international protestant church—at least the one recognized by the UN—has followed the structure of the Catholic church. It makes us easier to monitor."

I took the book from his hand. Its cover was an ancient-looking, dust-covered leather.

"Speaking of the Catholic church," Chris said, "this is an encyclical of Pope Alexander II. Few know of its existence. He was the pope who blessed William the Conqueror before he invaded England in 1066. He also had poignant visions and dreams, much like yours."

"You heard about those?" I asked.

"I did. Bart and I are leaders in the same order. We have been expecting you." He held up his glass. "Cheers to your mysteries."

My mysteries were none of his business, but I would drink to it nonetheless. "Cheers."

We clinked glasses and drank. I coughed as the drink burned down my throat.

"This is my best scotch," Chris said, "aged forty years."

"My dad drinks this stuff. Not bad. Is it older than you?"

"We're the same vintage." Chris smiled. Actually, he never stopped smiling. "Look, I know this all seems strange, and you're just here because you like Naomi." He winked at me. " She casts quite a spell."

I did not answer. I took another drink. It was smoother this time.

"I'll be honest with you," he continued, sounding serious for once. "We are very interested in your dreams. Bart will tell you more, but you should know it is very important. We believe the fate of the world may turn on...what?"

A laugh had slipped out of my lips. I couldn't help it— something about my dreams being tied to the fate of the world was too much. There had to be cameras in the room. This had to be a joke.

"I'm serious," he said.

"I can see that," I muttered. Maybe it was the drink loosening me up.

"Come." He took my arm hard enough to make me spill a few drops of scotch on his fancy rug. "I want to show you something." His tone made me stop laughing. He pulled me to his desk and touched his wrist to conjure a real-life image. It looked like the exact same tech I'd seen at ISA.

"Watch this," he said, "and we'll see if it's still funny. This video never went public."

The image sprang into motion. Chris was walking in his white robe. His smile was as wide as the ocean. It looked like he was in a slum, somewhere like Bombay or Bangladesh, probably a migrant camp after the flooding. Children were all around him, wearing rags and reaching out for him, as if his touch could rinse off their dirt and poverty. He kept on smiling and handing out food.

The image started to shake. Chris and the children staggered, losing their balance. Chris's face looked concerned, but then the shaking stopped and a moment later his perma-smile was back. He came to an older boy who stood in his path, holding up something. The screen spun and zoomed in on the paper the boy held, just as Chris took it in his hands.

My breath caught. It was a drawing of my dreams. The dragon was the same, and the man was standing before it. The setting was different, but everything else was just as I remembered it. Seeing the scenes from my mind take form on paper made it feel too real. How could this boy and I share the same vision? I took another drink.

Chris also took a sip, letting a moment of quiet hang in the air. He said softly, "I have seen dozens and dozens of these, from all over the world. I'd never seen anything like it before last year. Now they're everywhere." He was pointing behind me.

I turned around. One section of the bookshelves had spun open, revealing a gallery of drawings and paintings. Some were crude, like the poor boy's hand sketch. Others were oil paintings. A few were digitally-made images. The locations were all different, but the dragon and the man were the same in every single one.

"We must have all seen something that gave us these same images," I said. There was surely a reasonable explanation.

"Before your dreams, had you ever seen a creature like this springing from the earth?" Chris challenged.

"I'm not sure." Just because I didn't remember seeing it didn't mean it hadn't sneaked into my mind from somewhere.

"I think you *are* sure," Chris said. "And how about the man? Recognize him?"

I nodded, trying to keep my face blank. "I've seen him before. Don Cristo, the leader of the free world."

"And he showed up in dozens of dreams with this creature. What do you think that means?"

It had to be coincidence. "Maybe it means that a bunch of people saw the same movie or ad," I shrugged, "you know, with the President of the UN and some dragon creature."

He shook his head. He was not smiling. "These things do not happen by chance. We have been waiting for a Jewish boy from the Roeh line—a boy who has seen this vision in the Vatican. These things will come to be."

"You're serious," I said. "You really believe this? You know how crazy it sounds?"

"It's only crazy if it's not true. But this is true."

His certainty was unnerving. Did all of his underground order believe this? Did Naomi? It made sense that they would hide behind the façade of a megachurch with the stamp of government approval. "If it were true," I said, "wouldn't you be trying to tell the world?"

"That's not my role, Elijah. You look at me as if I'm the same man who preaches on broadcasts, as if I'm in this religious business for the fame and fortune. Good!" He sipped his scotch, and his smile was back. "That's how most look at me, and that's how I want it." He raised his glass to me. "Cheers to the true things, the things under the surface."

"Cheers," I said, more confused than ever. As our glasses clanked, I noticed the translucent ring on his thumb, just like Bart's. Who were these people?

He finished his drink in one big swallow, and I did the same. "Dinner calls," he said, studying me. "Tonight, no more talk of this conversation, or of what you saw here, okay?"

"Fine." I had a feeling I wouldn't get answers to my questions anyway. What I really wanted to know was Chris's motive. Was he just trying to unnerve me, or did he and his order actually think *I* was special? And could my growing knowledge of this order be used against me? The biggest secrets never stayed safe for long.

He led us out of the library, away from his collection of disturbing drawings.

We rejoined Naomi and Brie in the dining room. Naomi's warm voice welcomed us into casual conversation. We talked of Chris and Brie's children and other light topics as we ate. Chris never hinted at what he'd shown me, but the images kept tumbling through my mind.

Naomi and I said our goodbyes and left the mansion for the Cathedral. If what Chris had said was any indication, I could only imagine what I'd hear from Bart.

18

When we took our seats in Bart's crammed, medieval office, I felt almost comfortable. Maybe it was the scotch and the dinner resting in my belly, or maybe it was just being away from Chris. I could deal with Bart's craziness, or so I thought.

"You had the dream again?" Bart asked, his face glowing in the candlelight. His silver goatee and hair gleamed like sickles.

I nodded. I had vowed to myself that I would keep my words to a minimum. The goal was to satisfy Naomi. Besides, it was Bart's turn to talk.

"I was in it this time," Naomi volunteered. She sat beside me, on the edge of her chair as if she were about to watch a thriller. No one had brought popcorn.

"What did the man say?" Bart asked.

"He did not talk much," I answered. "How did you

know he spoke?"

He ignored my question. "What did he say?" he repeated.

"He told Naomi not to speak."

"What else?"

"He introduced himself and asked me to call him Don."

"Abaddon?"

I had already forgotten that name, but Bart was right. Had he heard that from the others who had similar dreams? "Yeah, Abaddon," I said. "Kind of sounds like an alien's name."

"Did you have any contact with him? Touch his hand?"

"No, I woke up before that."

Bart sighed and leaned back in his chair. He gazed up at the ceiling, where plaster was peeling and left odd shadows in the candlelight. His lips whispered something I could not hear. Then he leaned forward again and stared at me.

"Don't ever let him touch you." Bart rubbed his goatee as he spoke. "Elijah, you're going to have to be more open with me, but I suppose it's time for me to be more open with you, right?"

I hesitated before answering. It was not the kind of question with an easy answer. I had not bargained for any soul-bearing honesty from the crazy old monk. Naomi should have promised a kiss for that.

"You ever wonder why Naomi stays so quiet here?" Bart asked. Naomi smiled, but something seemed to be making her nervous. "She has a high calling," Bart continued. "She is on a mission. A mission to bring you—"

"Enough!" Naomi jumped to her feet. Bart cowered back in his chair. "Be honest about his dreams," she said, "and nothing more tonight."

Bart looked like a puppy caught peeing on the floor. He nodded slowly.

Naomi smoothed her dress and sat back down. I had never seen her speak with such force. Aisha's warning haunted me again. What mission was Bart talking about? Where was Naomi trying to *bring* me?

"My mission," Naomi said, putting her hand on my knee, "is to be with you now while we learn more about these dreams, to get some sleep tonight, and to pass our test tomorrow." She could probably see that I was not convinced.

"And tomorrow night?" I asked. Then we'd be on my terms. I put my hand over hers, and she did not pull away.

"Yes, tomorrow night." She smiled. "We'll talk more, at your secret location."

"Good, good," Bart interrupted. "Shall we get on with the story of your dreams?"

"Okay," I answered. The ticking clock behind Bart's desk showed 9:30 pm.

"This is a long story, a historical story." He chewed his lower lip with nervous excitement. "I'm afraid it's much too long for one night."

"Just an overview," Naomi said. "We can always come back to learn more. We have to be fresh for a test tomorrow."

"I will talk fast," Bart agreed. "Interrupt with any questions." He looked down at his desk and began tapping his fingers on a paper in front of him. "Where to begin, where to begin?"

His fingers stopped tapping. He leaned forward, folded his hands, and spoke to me. "It starts on an island in the Mediterranean, exactly two thousand years ago. The island was Patmos. It was not a place you wanted to be. There may have been beautiful days there, with views of the sea and a gentle breeze, but the Romans used the island as a prison. Only, it was not a prison for murderers and thieves. Those prisoners would do just fine in the grave or in a quarry outside the Empire's capital. This island was a prison for the worst threats to the Empire—traitors, demagogues, and zealots. These were the types the Romans could not risk having around others, or even killing. They fomented opposition. They stirred up disobedience. Romans could accept anything but that.

"And so the Romans could not accept a man named John. He was one of the men who had followed Jesus. In our faith, we call him an apostle. Are you familiar with him?"

"I've heard of Jesus," I said, maybe a little flippant.

Bart took a deep breath. "I'm not looking to waste your time or mine." It seemed he didn't like my tone.

"And I'm not looking for a sermon about Jesus." Maybe Naomi wouldn't like my tone either, but I didn't like where Bart was heading. "So we Jews killed him and you Gentiles worship him. Millions have died because of it. I thought our world had gotten beyond that. We agree to disagree about his or anyone else's divinity. Jesus was a wise dude, a prophet, a rabbi, a lunatic, whatever. Nothing else to say. Good enough?"

"I'll let you be the judge of that. I asked you a question." It seemed Bart's thick frame had a backbone in it. "Are you familiar with John?"

"Lennon? Yeah, he was a big deal a century ago."

Bart did not look amused. "To understand your dreams, you're going to need to learn more. I am trying to help."

He folded his hands over his belly and took another deep breath. "As I was saying, John was an apostle, and after Jesus died, John and others helped spread the word and the group of believers grew. They were like the Jews, refusing to accept the pantheon of Roman gods. The Romans could tolerate anything but an exclusive faith in a single God, kind of like the world today. For many years this group of Christians was a bunch of gnats hardly worth swatting. They sent letters between their tiny churches and their numbers grew. Eventually the gnats started to annoy Caesar. The Romans began killing the Christian leaders. They hanged one of them on an upside down cross. They cut off another one's head. They bludgeoned others with stones.

"Well, they tried to kill John, too, but he kept surviving. Legend says they dumped him in boiling oil but he lived. Then they tried something different. They shipped him off to Patmos. There he would be out of sight, out of mind, or so the Romans thought. I imagine John on Patmos was like a retired rock star at rehab."

I laughed. "Rock star?"

"Exactly," he said with a smirk. Then his face grew serious—as serious as the skull on his desk. "There was nothing pretty or funny about it. John craved friends and community, and his aging body could not handle the slave labor. His body bent and broke and burned under the hot Patmos sun. His mouth would be dry as the Sahara after a day of hauling stones on his back. After weeks of this work, John's body gave out. The Romans had gotten all they could from him, so they threw him into a guarded cave. They brought him water and flat bread once a day, just enough to keep him alive. He had lost everything, everything but his faith. He clung to his memories of Jesus like a baby clinging to its mother. He believed his faith would sustain him when nothing else would.

"Now, in this dark and miserable place, and with that pinprick of hope, John began to see things. He began to have dreams. He had visions. He saw beasts and dragons. He saw the earth splitting and cities crumbling. He saw the heavens opening. These were the kinds of things that would drive a normal man mad, but not John. He believed these visions were gifts from the Lord—glimpses into either the possible or the symbolic future.

"Not long after the visions began, a group of his supporters rescued him. They sailed to the island of Patmos in the dead of night, knocked out the guards, and took John into hiding. He told them all that he had seen and heard, and they wrote it down, getting the words just right. That was 66 AD, two thousand years ago."

"So...?" I'd done my part and listened. It wasn't clear what any of this had to do with me.

"So you're interested?" Bart had his big hand on an open book on his desk.

I glanced at Naomi. She had been quiet the whole time, but she still had not pulled her hand away from mine. She smiled at me now and squeezed my hand assuringly.

"It's an interesting story," I said.

"It's much more than a story." Bart picked the book up from his desk. "Here is what John wrote: *Then I saw an angel coming down from heaven, holding in his hand the key to the bottomless pit and a great chain. And he seized the dragon, that ancient serpent, who is the devil and Satan, and bound him for a thousand years, and threw him into the pit, and shut it and sealed it over him, so that he might not deceive the nations any longer, until the thousand years were ended. After that he must be released for a little while.*" Bart looked up at me with an edge in his eyes. "Who is the devil and Satan?"

"I have no clue," I said. I didn't mention that I doubted the devil even existed.

"You have every clue, because you have seen him."

"That's ridiculous."

"That's why you're here!" Bart suddenly clapped his hands. "Were you listening to me?"

"Yeah," I said, annoyed.

"I thought you were supposed to be a smart young man," Bart challenged. "Have you never heard the name

Abaddon before?"

"Other than my dream? No, I haven't. Why?"

"Listen to these words of John: *They have as king over them the angel of the bottomless pit. His name in Hebrew is Abaddon.*" Bart looked at me expectantly. "You're Jewish, right? Didn't you learn Hebrew?"

"A little, years ago." My mother had taught me, but those memories were dim. "So you're saying the man in my dream is the angel of the bottomless pit?" I would have found that amusing, except my dreams left little room for amusement.

"Yes!" Bart clapped his hands again. "Don't you see?"

I shook my head no. "If you made me guess, I would've picked the dragon."

"Our time is almost up, so I will be as clear as I can be." Bart grabbed a plain wooden cross from his desk and held it up to me. He spoke with reverence. "The devil, Satan, Abaddon, and whatever else this man has been called—he was bound, but he will be unbound and released for a little while. Some of his spirit enters a man, some of it is the pure, chaotic evil of a dragon. You have seen the beginning of what is to come. When *he* is unleashed, nothing else will matter. The world will be devastated. Earthquakes, storms, meteors, you name it."

"You know when this will happen?" Naomi asked with a touch of awe.

"No one knows," Bart said, "but I think it will be soon, very soon, this year, I believe. My order holds secrets. The secrets reveal signs. The signs hint at the time. But about that day or hour no one knows, not even the angels in heaven."

"Are we done?" I had heard enough and was feeling drained. I stood without waiting for an answer. It was a relief to be out of the stiff wooden chair.

"For now." Bart rose, walked around his desk, and opened the door. "But we will talk again, for you will have more dreams, Elijah."

Was that a threat?

"Bye Bart." Naomi put her slender arms around the priest's wide and round shoulders.

"Bye Naomi, you watch over him." He winked at her.

We were halfway out of the cathedral before I asked Naomi if Bart was always that crazy.

"Yes," she said, pausing to look at me, "and crazier yet, so far he's always been right." She put her hand softly on my shoulder. "Thank you, Elijah." Her face, her lips—they were beautiful as she spoke. "I know this is strange, but it means a lot that you heard Bart out. It's probably hard for you to believe, but *if* he's right, wouldn't that be worth knowing?"

That was hard to deny, but there was no way Bart was right. "I guess so," I shrugged off her question, "but I'm certain about one thing: you're worth knowing even if you have some rather unusual friends."

"And you're worth knowing even if you have some rather unusual dreams," she replied.

Touché, I thought. I did not say anything else about Bart or my dreams that night. I wouldn't question Naomi's faith if she wouldn't question my lack of it. Besides, I had earned tomorrow's date.

Next I just needed to ace an exam.

19

Friday, January 8. Test day.

Silent, intense delivery.

Instructor Wade had left those final words of guidance for the five of us. We had been told little of what this test would require, but we were to expect the unexpected, to stay silent unless commanded to speak, and to deliver results. He said we all had a good chance of passing, but there were no promises, and no preparation would help.

I faced most tests expecting perfection. My confidence was slightly shaken, though, by how little V had found about this one. She had also found nothing new in the report on Aisha and Naomi. I worried that someone or something was blocking information from my precept. Everyone knew ISA had the best hackers.

I set those worries aside. I would deliver with silence and intensity, and I would pass this test.

We were in the same large room where we'd had our simulations. Each of us sat far apart in an old-fashioned desk—the kind of desk without a single circuit, just a chair and a tray connected to it. The tray even had one of those little grooves to hold a pencil. I hadn't used a pencil since grade school, but there one was, sitting in front of me like a threat. Its point was shaved to precision. Its shaft was yellow and pure as it rested above the booklet. The booklet was a white stack of paper as thick as my thumb. The cover had two words in huge black letters:

TEST YOURSELF.

I assumed every breath would be watched and recorded. V was linked to the ISA-7 network. They had control. The test was all around us, not just in the booklet. I kept my gaze moving around the room, half expecting more androids to drop out of the ceiling and attack us. No robot came, only the Captain's voice. It spoke out of nowhere, as if it were just a thought in my mind.

Begin, his voice said. That was all.

I glanced around at the others. Charles and Patrick had already pulled open their booklets and were studying the words in it. Aisha stood up suddenly. Her chair had smoke coming from it, as if it was burning hot. She hopped onto the tray of her desk, kneeled down, and picked up her booklet. She opened it and began to read. Maybe burning chairs were part of her exam. Apparently we would each face our own challenges.

Naomi was looking at me when I turned to her. She smiled and playfully tossed her pencil into the air. It spun twice and she caught it. She pressed the eraser to her lips and mouthed the words, *it's on.* Her head turned to the booklet, which she pulled open with the delicacy of a bomb defuser.

I looked down again at the words before me.

TEST YOURSELF.

I opened the cover.

Welcome, Elijah. The first page was blank, but the words flicked into my mind. *Turn the page.* So I did.

The top of the next page said, "Circle the correct answer." There was a single multiple-choice question:

Which of James Madison's famous quotations is from Federalist Paper #10?

> A – "Ambition must be made to counteract ambition."
>
> B – "A standing military force, with an overgrown Executive, will not long be safe companions to liberty."
>
> C – "If men were angels, no government would be necessary."
>
> D – "Religion and government will both exist in greater purity, the less they are mixed together."

Rough start. Were they just messing with me? I had no clue what the answer was. They didn't teach that ancient stuff in school. V could have told me if I controlled her. I had at least heard of the "C" quotation, and "C" was always a good guess. But this was ISA-7. I did not trust a good guess. My instinct was to skip it for now, so I flipped the page.

Two points, said the Captain's voice in my mind. *None of the options were correct.*

On the next page, the word "SCREAM" was written in the middle. *Now yell "James Madison" as loud as you possibly can,* came the voice.

So much for silent delivery. I breathed in deeply and then let it out: "James Madison!"

Everyone in the room looked at me.

Zero points, the Captain said. *You were seventeen decibels short of your maximum capacity. Turn the page.*

Another multiple choice question.

Which factor contributed most to the U.S. invasions of Vietnam in the 1960s, Iraq in the 2000s, and Venezuela in the 2030s?

    A – Oil

    B – Absence of international leadership

    C – Conflicts with other superpowers

    D – Domestic politics

That one was easy. It looked like a question from a standard college admissions test. Every student was taught that the UN was the key to international peace. And the ISA was under UN control after all, no matter what ISA-7 did in secret. I circled B.

One point.

More and more questions and exercises followed, at least fifty total. I performed well, and I knew most of the answers. I did not know which company was the first to acquire sovereign territory when it claimed the moon, nor did I know who won the World Cup in 2026. But by the time I flipped to the booklet's last page, I was at eighty-seven points. Too bad I didn't know the grading scale.

As I looked at the last page, my hands started to shake. It was two pictures: Naomi's face beside Don Cristo's.

Scenario, began the Captain. *You and Naomi attend a banquet honoring the Premier of China. Your target is the precept of the President of the UN. Access and transfer his data. Estimated download time is five seconds. Secure the target at any cost. What do you do when this happens?*

Suddenly I shifted. I was in a palatial room with Chinese decor. It was like the simulations, except this time I was in my body, not in a drone. I was in a chair at an elaborate, long table with at least fifty others. The plate before me was empty except for the cracked shell of a lobster. Naomi sat to my right. Don Cristo sat across from her. I felt a small gun in my right pocket. Probably loaded with a tranquilizer.

"Pardon me," Cristo said to no one in particular. He stood and bowed gracefully in his tux. Then he walked off.

"Do not go," Naomi whispered. "It's a trap." She wore a stunning red dress and was made up like a movie star.

Was she actually in this simulation, or was someone else controlling her? I figured action was the only way to find out. "This might be our only chance," I said to her. "Follow me in one minute."

I stood and went after Don Cristo. His path led me through a door and then down wide, red-carpeted stairs. I glimpsed him entering another room at the end of a long hall. I rushed that direction. V told me Naomi had left her seat. So apparently they were letting V help me now.

I cracked open the door Cristo had entered. It was a men's restroom, full of marble and gold. I slipped inside.

Cristo was at a urinal, staring at the wall before him.

I raised my gun. It looked like it was loaded with a dart.

"I wouldn't do that," Cristo said calmly. He still faced the wall. "She'll die if you do. Go ahead, peek outside."

"Don't move," I demanded. I cracked the door open again. Naomi was there, surrounded by dozens of soldiers with guns aimed at her. She had her hands up.

Our eyes met for a moment. It wasn't really her, was it?

I looked back inside. Cristo had turned to face me. He was smiling.

"Fire now!" he shouted.

I fired just as other gunshots rang out.

Cristo stumbled to a knee. I glanced back toward Naomi. She was doubled over, hands on her side, staring at me.

"Elijah," she groaned. "Help me." She reached out with a blood-covered hand, and then fell forward.

I stepped towards her, more gunshots erupted, and then everything went black.

I was in my desk again. The only one still in the room.

Eighty-seven points, said the Captain's voice in my head. *End of examination. Report here at noon tomorrow for results.*

20

When I left the room, Naomi was waiting for me.

"How'd it go?" she asked cheerfully. There was no red dress, no blood. It was just Naomi, looking like a model in a blue thrift-shop jumpsuit.

"I'm not sure," I said. I didn't know what else to say.

"Well, it's done, right?" She took my hands. "Is everything okay? What happened?"

"Nothing. It was just an interesting test."

"You can say that again. So, where are you taking me? When do we leave?"

"Are you ready?" I asked. I needed to get out of this building and out of the city. Maybe that would help clear my head.

"Do I need to take anything?" She looked down at her clothes. "I like to be comfortable when I take tests, but I'm guessing this is underdressed?"

"No problem, I've arranged for that. And you always look amazing anyway. Let's go now."

She smiled. "You lead the way."

As we made our way outside, I instructed V to rent a sports car and spare no expense. It showed up in the Pentagon parking lot five minutes after we walked out. It was the perfect vehicle—black composite carbon, solar wings, and remote drive.

We jumped in and rode to a town called Warrenton before the auto-drive stopped. The car pulled off the highway and into a transition station. The steering wheel folded out of a compartment in front of me.

I put my hands on the wheel. It would feel good to actually drive. "We're almost there," I told Naomi.

"A boy from Manhattan driving manual?" Naomi put her hand beside mine on the wheel. "You sure you don't want me to drive?"

I smiled at her, then slammed my foot on the pedal. Naomi slid her hand away and pressed back into her seat. We were flying down the road in seconds, the leafless trees passing in a blur.

"My family has a few places in the country," I said once we were cruising. "One of them is near the Finger Lakes in New York. I spend my summers there, driving on roads a lot like this." The remnants of the city were behind us. Gentle hills rolled before us toward a blue ridge of mountains in the distance.

"Summers at your lake house?" Naomi asked. "Sounds nice. I'm guessing you spend your winter breaks at a Swiss chalet?"

"How'd you know?" Our chalet was in France, but just across the border in the alps. She was close enough. "This year I'm missing the slopes so I can be here, you know, taking tests and serving our country."

"Some sacrifice," Naomi laughed. "All I'm missing is my holiday reading." She paused. "I know you've been avoiding this, but how do you think you did on the test?"

"I'm not sure," I said. "In the end, I had eighty-seven points. How about you?"

"I didn't get a number."

"Really? What did your precept say when it was over?"

"It said 'completed' and told me to report back tomorrow for the results."

"Interesting." Now I was worried. It made no sense for me to get a number and for her to just "complete." What if she had failed it? All I said was, "I guess we'll find out tomorrow then."

"That we will," she replied in a carefree tone.

The first sign for the Inn at Little Washington was ahead. "Don't you want to know where we're going?" I asked.

"Somewhere obscenely expensive, I'm guessing. And you're paying double so I can have my own room, right?"

"Yes and yes," I answered. "It's a little inn in a little town, but it has quite a history."

"Hmm...I've heard of only one place around here that meets that description. You're not kidding about your wealth."

I shrugged. "I'm hoping to buy you the best dinner of your life. We've earned it after this week."

"That sounds nice, as long as you're not trying to repeat history," she warned. "You must know this little inn has hosted its share of controversy."

"It adds character," I said, "unless you're the president, I guess."

"You could say that," she scoffed. "I never liked President Thorne, but from what I hear, he had good taste for where to wine and dine his mistresses."

I smiled. "It can't be an affair if neither of us is married."

"Not funny."

"Sorry. I promise, the only history we'll be repeating is some of the finest dining in the world." I slowed to turn off the main road. "Just a couple minutes now."

We passed another modest sign.

"So it *is* the Inn at Little Washington," she said, sounding as excited as I'd hoped. "I can't wait to see the table where Thorne was caught. Can you believe that was just nine years ago? I heard prices doubled after the scandal."

"All press is good press." I took the final turn toward the small and perfect country inn.

"It's beautiful," she said with a hint of wonder.

"It's fitting for a night like this," I replied, as we came to a stop. *Fitting*, I thought, because it was outside her comfort zone. How else was I going to figure out whether to heed Aisha's warning? I also needed to check my feelings for Naomi. It had been a very confusing week.

Two bellmen opened our doors. A rush of cool air blew in. We were outside the warming shield of the capital.

"Welcome, Mr. Goldsmith," said one of the men. "It is a pleasure to see you again. Come, we have everything ready."

They whisked us inside. The day's exam and the week's stress began to melt away in the face of luxury. The lobby smelled of herbs and cedar-burning fire. The white-gloved receptionist welcomed us and told us our room numbers. The rooms were already synced with our precepts. Naomi and I parted, with a plan to meet in an hour for dinner.

21

I could not have drawn it up any better.

Naomi sat across from me at the immaculate dinner table. She wore the dress I'd asked to have waiting in her room. V had found her size, and the Inn's staff had excellent taste. The dress was slim and red and perfect. Perfect except for the flicker of memory it brought back from the test. She was just as stunning as she'd been in the simulation.

I had done my best to match her, with a light grey tux. I'd even worn the bowtie. My dad would have been proud. He had once told me that, if I wanted to impress someone, dinner at the Inn was one of life's only sure bets. For once I was glad I'd followed his advice.

While the first courses were served, Naomi and I talked about the week and ISA-7. By the time the entrée arrived, our conversation was relaxed and easy. I was enjoying her company, instead of trying to figure everything out.

But then she asked, "What are you doing on April 17?" She was halfway through her filet mignon. She had savored each bite, as if it were a last meal.

"Probably skipping class, maybe going to a party, about to graduate," I said. "Why? What day of the week is that?"

"It's a Saturday." Her eyes were an invitation. "I'm hoping you might be my date for a wedding that day."

"That should work," I said, "and I'd be honored." It would at least keep us connected outside ISA. A tiny part of me had worried she'd forget about me once we left training—kind of like how my dad always forgot about me if we weren't in the same room. Besides, I could always skip a couple days of class, and this would be my best excuse yet. "Where is it?" I asked. "Who's getting married?"

"It's a friend of mine, Jade Taylor. She lives in New Zealand. We met when I studied abroad there a couple years ago."

"So the wedding is on the other side of the world?" *Interesting,* I thought. New Zealand had not shown up in V's report on Naomi. I hid my surprise behind a bite of buttery sea bass.

"Actually, the wedding is in the Vatican." She hesitated. "In St. Peter's Basilica."

"Seriously?" A shiver ran down my spine. "You know what I've dreamed about that place. How does anybody get married there anyway?"

"Jade's family is close with the Cardinal from New

Zealand. They're old money, like you." She leaned forward, her lips playfully pouty. "You keep saying these dreams are just dreams. Prove it. Come with me."

Something in my gut warned me to say no, that my dreams were not just dreams. Why else would Naomi invite me? I wanted to think it was just because she liked me, but I remembered Bart's words about her mission to *bring* me somewhere. Still, dragons didn't exist. What happened in my dreams was impossible. And she was right; there was no way to prove it except by showing up.

"I'll come," I said. If my life had a soundtrack, I figured someone would've just banged an ominous gong.

Her face lit up like a sunrise. "Wonderful! So will you also come a week early for Easter? It's the Sunday before. I've heard there's nothing like Easter at the Vatican."

"You're pushing your luck. Remember?" I pointed to myself. "Jewish kid. We take to Easter like cats take to water." I hid my unease at the thought of thousands gathered in the Vatican piazza, listening to the Pope. It was eerily close to what I'd seen. "Plus, that would mean skipping a whole week of school just before graduation."

"Please, for me? It's not like they'll keep you from graduating."

She was right again, but that did nothing to settle my unease. "What if I skipped out on Easter and joined you only for the wedding?" I asked.

She studied me with a smile. "You're nervous, aren't you? Think Bart might actually be right?"

I felt myself losing ground in this conversation. "Well, I

never guessed I'd be in the Vatican anytime soon. That doesn't mean Bart's right, but it is a little strange."

"What if he's right? Wouldn't you want to find out? And if he's wrong and Easter passes as it has for a couple millennia, then we'll travel to Tuscany during the week before the wedding. You can pick the hotels. You can even pick my clothes, like you did tonight." She ran her hands along the red silk fabric, drawing my eyes down the slightly open front and towards her exposed honey skin. "So? Are you in?"

Two images competed in my head. One was the piazza packed with people, an earthquake, a dragon rising from the ground, and Don Cristo saying my name. The other was like a scene from a Renaissance painting—perfect green hills, a beautiful hilltop town, and Naomi smiling and laughing with my hand around her waist. I was always a sucker for the Renaissance. Between the dreams and Naomi, I had to take Naomi.

"Okay, I'll go." I finished my wine, pretending to be cool. This time my soundtrack was rumbling thunder in the distance.

Excitement filled Naomi's voice as she told me more about her friend Jade, the wedding, and the Vatican. We ate dessert while she explained about the Pope who took his position a couple decades ago. He led the tiny nation to remain one of the few holdouts from the UN's global telecom system. She told me no one in the Vatican even had precepts. Everything she said was interesting. Everything about her was interesting.

After dinner, we found an isolated sitting room with a soft leather couch and a crackling fire. I sat close to her, our knees touching. At some point I put my hand on hers. I was losing all track of time. The fire was burning low before my final thread of caution broke. I could not let this night drift into a tepid ending.

I met her eyes. "I wouldn't think a girl like you would invite a guy like me to a wedding in a foreign country."

"You're not like other guys." The firelight made her face glow. "And don't you know by now that I'm not easy to predict?"

"Hard to predict, yes." Her magnetic pull compressed the space between our eyes. "You're not like anyone else I've met."

She tilted her head back slightly, drawing me forward.

My heart was racing as I leaned closer. Her soft lips were inches from mine.

I went for the kiss.

But she moved back.

Then she pressed her lips to my forehead. My heart sank to my feet. My unheard soundtrack jarred to a stop. Her hand was on my flushed cheek.

"Thank you for tonight," she said, smiling warmly. "The best things wait until they're unexpected. Let's see what Rome brings." Her kiss was a feather's touch on my cheek before she stood. "Goodnight, Elijah."

I stood. "Goodnight, Naomi." My voice was surprisingly steady, given I felt like I'd just swallowed a gallon of awkwardness.

She turned to go. Her figure was like a thin candle flame as she walked away.

I fell back onto the couch and stared at the fire. I had been so caught up in her that I'd forgotten to ask that we sync our precepts, as if she would have accepted. It hardly seemed to matter. My head did not stop spinning until it found a deep, dreamless sleep.

22

The next morning, a dense fog laid heavy over the countryside. Naomi and I had breakfast together and left the Inn. We talked more of the wedding in April while we drove back to the city. She acted as if we were closer than ever. She even reached for my hand once the auto-drive picked up. Maybe she felt bad about the dodged kiss. It just made me feel sick to my stomach.

As we drew closer to Washington, a sense of dread began to rise inside me. I wondered if it was because of some dream I'd had but could not remember, or the wedding trip to Rome, or maybe just the fog. When you can't see what's a hundred feet ahead, everything in the future starts to feel like a threat.

We arrived at the ISA building at 11:30. I hesitated before getting out of the car.

Naomi looked at me with curiosity. "You ready?"

"Mostly," I said. "But I don't want to go back in there as if nothing has changed." I met her eyes. "What are we going to be after this week is over?"

She smiled. "I don't know, Elijah, but it's clear there's *something* between us."

"You didn't act like it last night," I said.

"But I *did*, for me," she said. "It's been an intense week. I don't want to rush into anything."

"You mean, like inviting me to a wedding in Rome?"

"That's different."

"How?"

"I could invite any friend to a wedding."

Any friend—that stung. "So I'm just a friend who has some dreams you want to test? Is that it?"

"No," she sounded hurt, confused. "I like you...more than I should. I really do, but you have to admit, we have some major differences."

"So why should I come to the wedding?"

"Because maybe it will help us get past the differences."

"You really believe that?"

She nodded, but I needed more.

"I'll prove my interest by going," I said, "but you have to prove yours, too."

"Okay," she said, "how?"

"Sync with me."

"I'm not sure about that."

No surprise there. "Why not?"

"It's not you," she said, pressing her lips together uncertainly. "But isn't that a little fast? And what about

ISA-7, don't you think they would notice?"

"Why would they care? It would just make it easier for them to make us partners. We have to leave DC and each other today, you know. Don't you think we'll feel isolated once we go back to regular life? We'll have access to all this information and technology, but we won't be able to share it, except with each other."

"Who else would you want to share it with?" she asked.

"I don't know," I shrugged. "Other friends?"

"You mean your friends from school? You never talk much about them."

"I guess you never asked," I said, but the truth was I didn't have close friends. I had V, which was usually good enough...until Naomi came along. "Look," I said, "I don't want to lose the *something* we've started. Let's keep a piece of each other, okay?"

She thought for several moments, with no emotion on her face. I felt sure she would say no. But she surprised me. "Okay," she said, "we can sync if you promise no judging. We won't have time to view or talk about our information before we go in for the test results."

"Understood," I said. "No judging."

I held out my wrist.

She pressed her wrist to mine.

"Sync," I said.

"Sync," she echoed.

Our precepts began to speak in unison: "Five, four, three, two, one. Sync complete."

Then it was done. I now carried all her biometrics in

my precept, in my mind. I summoned my map screen through V. Naomi was a blinking green dot beside me. I shifted to a status screen. Her body temperature was 99.2 degrees. She'd eaten 743 calories this day. Her web of networks was vast. I noticed a few in Italy, so I check them. They were locked. I checked the ones in DC. Locked. There were thousands across the world, but I had a feeling all their identities were hidden from me, password-protected.

Her pulse was rising. And she knew mine was, too. I suddenly felt naked with her knowing so much about me, all at once.

I shut off the screen. Naomi's cheeks were flushed. There was a tinge of doubt, almost fear, in her eyes.

"No judging," I assured her.

She nodded. "We have to go now. Let's get water on the way. We both need hydration."

Of course we did. Maybe I would have to start eating better. "How do you know so many people?" I asked.

"Some information stays hidden for a reason." She opened her car door. "We can't show all our secrets at once," she said, some of her confidence returning.

We both stepped out. The world was the same, except now Naomi and I were linked together in it.

23

Naomi and I hurried to the ISA-7 room. Our three classmates were already there, waiting for the results of the exam. The looks on their faces were telling as they saw Naomi and me entering together. Patrick looked like a sad puppy. Charles grinned like a prankster. And Aisha looked concerned and brooding. I had not had a chance to ask Charles about Aisha's message.

"We missed you at the movie last night," Charles said.

"What did you see?" Naomi asked.

"*Lost in China*," Charles answered. "It's a story of boy meets girl, except this time the boy is a Chinese prison guard and the girl is an American who was taken during the attack in '53. It was pretty good, but no Oscar."

"Charles left out one part," Aisha chimed in. "His mom was in it! She played the mom of the Chinese boy. Can you believe he hadn't told us she was an actress?"

Charles shrugged. "That's what precepts are for."

"Where do you think he got his good looks?" I asked.

"I worked hard for it," Charles said, running a hand through his hair like a model and making the group laugh. He knew how to lighten a mood, but mine was still dark.

"How was your trip to the country?" Patrick asked Naomi, as if the rest of us were not standing there.

"It was very nice," Naomi said with a straight face. Only I knew her pulse ticked up at Patrick's question. It made me smile. "Sometimes it's good to get away before a big day like today," she added. "Any news about the results?"

"We saw Wade in here a few minutes ago." Charles glanced over his shoulder into the room, and then continued in a mockingly low voice. He knew they'd hear what he said no matter how quietly he whispered. "Wade says four of us passed."

"Four?" Naomi's eyebrows lifted like rainbow arcs.

Four, the Captain's voice came into my mind through the ISA-7 network. From the looks on the others' faces, they had heard it, too. *Take your seats.*

We obeyed the order and sat in our chairs. We were lined up before a huge screen. A panel in the floor slid away, and the Captain rose up to face us.

"Four of you passed," he said, as the floor sealed shut and the screen came on. "That's pretty good. I figured, with your group, two or three might make it on the first try."

He turned his back to us and gestured to the screen. An image of the blue-and-white UN flag appeared, rippling as if in a gentle wind. I had never seen it so big. It covered the whole wall of glass and was five times the height of the Captain. The man stood motionless, a small silhouette staring at the image before us.

"This is why you came here. To protect our world." He turned to face us, his voice almost emotional. "Once you step through the door of ISA-7, there is no turning back. We are the invisible front line. If we stop a threat, no one knows about it. If a threat passes through us, tragedy will come. We give up freedom so that we can be freedom's best hope." He stepped closer to us. "You have heard all this. You know the stakes. But before you know if you passed, you must know that passing means you step across a threshold of no return. It's time to affirm your commitment."

He moved to face Patrick, to the far left from me. He stood there silently, holding Patrick in a stare.

"What words do I need to say?" Patrick asked.

"The pledge," the Captain answered. He sounded like a patient father. He'd never sounded like that before.

Patrick put his hand over his heart. "I pledge allegiance to the flag—?"

The Captain nodded. He almost looked proud.

"To the flag," Patrick continued, "of the United Nations, and to the security for which it stands, one world indivisible, with liberty and justice for all."

The Captain then stepped to Aisha. She said the pledge. Then Charles, Naomi, and I each did the same.

"We will meet again," the Captain saluted us. "It will be

an honor to fight alongside you." He went back to the spot on the floor that lowered him down and out of sight.

Wade rushed in after that. The enormous flag was still behind him. "Okay y'all, it's about time for the results. If you pass, you'll receive a percentage score, and we use that to place you within our ranks. We'll have sessions this afternoon about your first orders. And remember, even if you don't pass today, you are still in ISA." He glanced towards me. "You can test again for ISA-7."

My heart began to race. Was his glance supposed to mean that I had failed? I looked to Naomi by my left side. She smiled and nodded. For once it was little comfort.

"Here you go," Wade said. He pressed his wrist.

A word dropped like an anvil on my head: *Failed.*

24

It took me a moment to remember where I was. This was the ISA-7 training room. My classmates were beside me. I realized none of them had heard the word in my mind. Their faces were focused, as if they were hearing a message.

All I heard was the echo of the word: *Failed.*

Wade came to me. He took my arm gently and helped me out of the chair. We walked beside each other. He opened the door and guided me out. I had not had a chance to say anything to the others. They had passed the exam. They were moving on.

"I know this is hard," Wade was saying. "Your time will come. It took me four tries to pass, but here I am now."

He was no comfort. I was not Wade. I had never failed, not like this.

He kept talking as he led me out of the building. He

was saying something about more chances, hard work, and sticking with it. I barely heard him.

We left the building and he stayed beside me. I wondered how far he was going to escort me. Maybe I was a threat to ISA-7 now. Maybe I knew too much.

Once we were within eyesight of my hotel, he stopped. "Listen to me, Elijah."

"I'm listening."

"I'm not supposed to say much," he said, "but you should know you were close. If it were just your abilities, you would already be in. You would be one of our best." He put a finger to my temple. "But you have some disturbing images in your mind. You may want to see someone, you know, work those things out. We'll test again this summer. We start the first Monday in July. Can I count on you being here?"

I said nothing. Did he really expect me to commit now? Maybe the Captain was right. Maybe this was a sign—a sign that I was not the type to give up my freedom to serve. That was what my dad had said all along. Was it really worth all this to prove him wrong?

"Naomi will be here again in July," Wade said.

"Why does that matter?" I fired back.

He leaned away. I realized I had shouted louder than I'd intended. Losing my temper was no help, but that didn't stop me. Reason succumbs to shock and failure.

"I will be seeing her before then," I said, grasping for anything that made me feel competent.

Wade nodded with an amused grin. "We know more

than you think, Elijah. Sometimes pairs team up for our missions. When two people sync closely, it can be more risky to keep them apart. We've never seen a sync as powerful as yours and Naomi's. But now she can share ISA-7 information only with those on her team and her reporting authorities. You won't be able to talk to her about her most important work, and we'll know if she relays something she shouldn't."

I knew a threat when I heard one. He was right, though. The secrecy of ISA-7 would be a wedge between us. Already V showed that Naomi was downloading a trove of protected data, as she sat in the same room where we'd gotten the results. The sync almost made it worse—I *knew* how much I couldn't know about Naomi's new information.

"I'll be here," I told Wade. "First Monday in July." That was half a year away. It didn't hurt to say the words. I could always change my mind.

"Excellent!" Wade raised his forearm toward me. "Lift your arm, please?"

I did, and he tapped his arm against my wrist.

"I just gave you the debrief package," he said. "Don't be too hard on yourself. At least one person fails every time. You still have what it takes for ISA-7. You have more than that."

I nodded, even though it didn't help to hear that someone always fails, not when that someone was me.

"See you on July fifth!" Wade said, as if it were the date of a kid's birthday party.

Then he walked away and left me alone.

I went to my hotel room, shut off V and everything else, and laid facedown on the bed. I could not come up with any explanations. My thoughts were all meaningless and miserable. My classmates' faces kept appearing. I imagined them laughing at me, except Naomi's face was sad. That was even worse. Our sync was no comfort.

V would have to stay disconnected for a while, even if that left the world more bland. I could not bear a fast and colorful mind in my state. Sometimes slow and monotone thinking was not so bad.

I tried to find solace in my return to school. It would be my last semester before graduation, and I could look forward to college in the fall. Maybe I'd fit in a ski trip in the Alps, or I'd join my dad in the tropics. Naomi and I could travel together in Italy. Good distractions, but this pain was here to stay. I had failed, and failed spectacularly.

I eventually fell asleep. Then a dream came. It was a lucid dream, the kind you have only during a bleak midday nap.

25

"Don't go," said the man with solid black eyes.

"He must go," said the woman with Naomi's eyes.

"He cannot go. She will die."

"That is a lie."

"As true a lie as you've ever heard."

I was standing between the man and the woman as they talked. We were in an empty space. The only colors were black to one side and white to the other. I stood where the black and white met, like straddling the line down a yin-yang.

"Death is temporary in this place." The woman was standing on the side of me with only white in the distance. Her wispy robe was the same blank color. She had long blond curls and traces of wrinkles at the corners of her green Naomi-eyes.

"This is about more than life or death. It is about *him*."

The man on the black side of me was not frightening, despite his eyes. He was magnificent, with shimmering white opal skin and long black hair falling over his high black collar. "Are you so brave," he asked the woman, "that you'll let him touch the world—*touch her*—so that he can enter fully?"

"Who is *he*?" I asked.

The man glanced down at me, with a stunning, expressionless face. "Look who woke up," he said. "It's about time you let your eyes see and your ears listen." His stare filled me with nervous excitement, as if great pleasure awaited. "*He* is the man you've seen, the man from your dreams."

"Don?"

The woman laughed lightly. "Is that what he calls himself now? His name is Abaddon." Her face became stern. "You cannot let him touch you. Only you can see what must be seen. You must protect her when he comes, and after he comes."

"Who must I protect?" I asked.

"You already know what you should not," said the man.

"The woman clothed with the sun," added the woman. "Nations rise and fall, but the word is truth about what is to come. But oh, how *he* will twist it." She sounded deeply sad, on the verge of tears. "You must go, and you must protect her."

The woman's sadness infiltrated me. It had power over me. I would have done anything to make her smile. "I will try," I said, "but how can I protect her if *he* will touch her?"

"You cannot go." The man placed his fingers under my chin and gently turned my face to his. "She will die if you go. Her blood will be on your hands. Why would you give up all that you have before you in this life?"

He was right, or at least his words made me want to believe he was right. His presence was like an invitation to swim in the pleasures of my existence, to live a life of only the finest happiness on earth.

"You must go," the woman repeated. She was drifting away from me, into the infinite white space. "Do not let him touch you." Her words grew faint.

"Do not go." Now the man was drifting away, too, in the opposite direction of the black. "Think of what you will lose."

Then I was alone, straddling the divide of black and white. I felt compelled to take a step, but I could not decide which direction. The weight of the decision was more than I could bear. I didn't even know what the decision was.

I opened my eyes. I was on my bed in the hotel room. Someone was knocking on the door. I stood and walked to it, my mind still stuck in the strange space between the man and the woman.

The knock came again, insistent. I pulled the door open.

It was Naomi.

She took me into her arms before I had a chance to think. I leaned my head on her shoulder and closed my eyes. Her shoulder was the perfect height.

"I'm so sorry," she was saying. "I know you will pass next time. How are you?" She wore real concern on her face. "You turned off your precept."

I looked into her eyes. The eyes that were just like the woman's eyes. Had it really been just a dream?

"I'm fine," I said.

"You're a terrible liar. You'll need to work on that if you want to rise to the top of ISA." She took my hands in hers. "Here, let's practice. Tell me a lie."

"You're ugly," I said. "I don't like being around you."

"That's two lies! But, yes, that's good." She paused. "Here's one: I would never invite a boy to a wedding if he failed the ISA-7 exam."

"I could never date a spy."

"And I could never date a Jew."

"Christians freak me out."

"I win!" she announced. "That's no lie. I know my friends freak you out."

That was true enough. I suddenly thought of the man in black from the dream. *You cannot go*, he'd said. Maybe he was right. Maybe I was falling too fast for her. I needed time to think.

"I'm leaving tonight," I said.

"Won't you stay for the team dinner?" She squeezed my hands in plea.

"I'm not on the team anymore. Maybe next time."

"Okay." She took my face in her hands and looked deep into my eyes. "When will we see each other next? I don't want to wait until April."

"I'll visit you." The words came out of my mouth without thought. *You must protect her*, said the woman in white. Great, now I was hearing voices. I tried to stay calm. "When works for you?" I asked, as casually as I could.

"How about in February? Second weekend?"

"February it is."

"And we'll be in touch before that."

"Every day," I said, "once I reconnect my precept anyway. We're synced."

"You make that sound sensual." She leaned closer to me. "You're an interesting boy, Elijah."

She pecked my lips, lingering a blissful moment and making me forget for a moment all about ISA-7 and exams and dreams and the world. When she pulled back, I realized I was smiling for the first time all day.

"This week has been—" she began.

"*Something*," we said together.

My first weeks back at boarding school were like a long hangover. I made it two days before I reconnected V. I talked to Naomi every day after that. I could check her location and her body temperature any time, but it was not the same. Our week together had come and gone and left in its wake my failure on the ISA-7 exam.

Classes and senior-year parties were not much help. That one week with Naomi felt more important than all of it. I wondered if such a small stretch of days could outweigh the rest of my life. I wondered why my dreams had gone blank. I wondered whether they had meant anything after all.

At least today I had a new distraction. It was the first Sunday of February, Super Bowl Sunday. I didn't care about football, but if I was going to attend a game, it might as well be the hundredth Super Bowl. The World Football

League was making this more than just a football game. It was a party, a festival, and a worldwide extravaganza to celebrate the centennial. No other city but my hometown could have been fitting as the site, especially with the New York Giants playing.

I'd stayed in my family's place the night before. My dad was in Geneva on some urgent business. Nothing new there, but that's why he'd given me his two tickets. I probably could have bought a parcel on the moon with them, but I already had one of those. Might as well go and see the spectacle.

Now I was waiting for Charles, which was odd. He was never late like this. I had a lot of valid reasons for inviting him. He was a friend. He was fun. Like me, he didn't really care about the football. He'd be interested to watch the Shanghai Dragons play. This was the first time a Chinese team had reached the Super Bowl since they joined the league years ago. I was hoping Charles could also tell me more about where'd he been and what he'd been doing with ISA-7. I'd barely seen him since returning to school.

Those were all valid reasons, which made it even easier to hide the true reason for giving Charles my other ticket. I needed to understand the warning about Naomi. I still had no clue why Charles had passed the message through Aisha, or why he'd wanted to warn me in the first place. The two times I'd tried to bring it up, he'd come up with some excuse to leave. I figured the Super Bowl was a great way to make him sit beside me for a few hours. It was a promising sign that he'd accepted without hesitation.

But now he was late, really late. The crowd around me was getting smaller, with almost everyone already in the stadium or on their way. I checked with V again. No messages. Naomi was still in North Carolina. Nothing unusual about her stats.

I blinked the screen off and gazed out toward the new stadium. It was across the water, on Governor's Island just south of Manhattan. Thin bridges like spider legs connected the stadium to the surrounding boroughs. A rainbow of neon lights lit the bridges, making every ripple of water shimmer in green and orange and blue, as if a layer of oil floated on the surface. It gave the water a dream-like feel. If I'd had any dreams since the ISA week, I hadn't remembered a single one. I almost missed them. At least they'd brought something unexpected and unexplainable into my life.

"Elijah!" shouted Charles from behind me.

I turned and saw him rushing towards me. He was wearing a red jersey with an ornate golden serpent on the chest. His hair was matted as if he'd just taken off a helmet. The smile on his face did not reach his eyes.

"So sorry I'm late," he said, out of breath. "I grabbed dinner with some cousins in China Town. Once they found out I was going to the game, they wouldn't let me go until they found a jersey for me."

"No problem." I pointed to the Giants logo on my blue jersey. "We're going to look a bit odd sitting beside each other, but I still got your back if someone picks a fight."

"Ha, thanks!" he said. "If someone wants to pick a

fight, let's trade jerseys. You know better than anyone, my good Asian looks don't mean I actually cheer for the Shanghai Dragons."

"You think that'll stop these fans?"

"I thought the real fans were priced out of this game."

"Good point," I said. "This is a different crowd."

"Well, whoever starts something with me, I'll give them a Kung Fu ass kicking." He boxed at the air, followed by a high kick. His movements were sharp and strong, particularly for a guy like Charles. Maybe ISA-7 included some Kung Fu training.

"So very American of you," I joked. "Come on, let's go or we'll miss the whole game."

It was almost halftime when we entered the stadium and made our way down to our seats. We were about ten rows up, on the fifty-yard line.

"What do you want to drink? Any food?" I asked Charles as we sat.

"No food, but something Chinese and potent to drink." He smiled as the Giants fan beside us gave him a questioning look. "Looks like the Dragons need to rally."

I checked the score hovering over the middle of the field. The Giants were up 28-24. "Remember Charles, it's *go Giants* tonight." I pressed my wrist to the side of my seat and ordered two beers. The drinks showed up moments later, rising on a platform through a small hole that opened at our feet. We took the cups and the platform dropped back through the floor.

The lights suddenly dimmed for the halftime show.

Lasers of color began beaming around the stadium. A section of the grass slid open, and a stage rose to the sound of deep rumbling bass. Hundreds of scantily-clad dancers sprang into motion over the entire field. In the center was a Chinese boy band paired with America's newest pop diva. They started some sort of sing-off, dance-off. The tune was catchy.

I turned to Charles, ready to make some quip, but his face stopped me dead. He looked pale.

"What's wrong?" I asked. I wondered for a second whether his beer was poisoned.

He slowly mouthed the words, "precept off," without a sound leaving his lips.

I commanded it off. "What's going on, man?" No one around was paying us any attention.

He leaned his head close to mine and whispered in my ear, "*Don't go.*"

"Where?" I asked. "What are you talking about?"

"Quiet," he demanded. "They're listening."

"Who?" Even if someone was listening, they weren't hearing anything. I could barely hear Charles over the music, even though he was speaking straight into my ear. All the other fans were staring at the performance on the field.

"ISA!" he snapped. He pulled my head lower, into a huddle, and spoke fast. "Listen to me, Eli. The Chinese agents are pulling back, even from their strongest bases in the Middle East. They've left no one in Iran. They know something we don't, and ISA knows pretty much everything. ISA-7 has a few tricks up its sleeve, but I can't risk telling you too much. You've got to retake the test and get in. Then you'll know. But for now, don't go anywhere with Naomi. Not North Carolina, not Rome. Got it?"

I most certainly did not get it, and the fact that he knew about Rome put me on edge. I'd never heard Charles talk like this. It didn't even sound like him. "Why not?" I challenged. "You cheered me on. Now you tell me to stay away? That's like staying away from oxygen."

Charles cut me off. "This is no joke!"

"I'm not joking," I said. "You know how I feel about her. She and I are synced, man."

"Then sever the sync, and stay away from her. You know about her cult?"

"Yeah, I met some of them. They're weird, but from everything I've seen, they're harmless."

"Then you haven't seen enough," he said. "They're a huge threat, mixed up in a dangerous game. They've got agents in China and everywhere else. They're playing every side, meddling with rulers, working against the UN. Whatever the Chinese agents know, whatever they're retreating from, you don't want to be around when it hits."

"When what hits, and around where?" I asked. He wasn't making any sense.

"Around Naomi!" His face twisted into rage, then it was blank an instant later. "Trust me, for your own good."

I met his blank stare with my own. The last thing he was doing was earning my trust, but it was no good telling him that. I figured I might as well make him think I believed him. "Alright, man. But what is the danger? What's going to *hit*? Can't you give me a little more info?"

"I'm telling you all I can," he said, with too much conviction. What was he holding back? "You're my friend, Eli. I had to warn you about Naomi and her order. They're playing you, like everyone else. Don't go to Rome."

Rome again? Had Naomi told him? Was the order really a threat? As the questions raced through my mind, I nodded at Charles with my best attempt at sincerity. "I'll think about it," I said, leaning back in my chair.

"Don't think. *Act* on it," he insisted. "This is the most important game ever."

As if on cue, the stadium lit up and the crowd burst into applause. Whatever had impressed them, I'd missed it.

"Some show!" Charles said as if we'd never had the conversation a moment before. He didn't bring it up again, and neither did I.

He had revealed more than I'd hoped, but everything about it was odd. Nothing about it was concrete. Just veiled threats and risks. It would take more than that to keep me away from Naomi. Even if she gave me some doubts, couldn't I trust her more than Charles?

We watched the rest of game like normal football fans. I pretended to enjoy the beer, cheerleaders, and competition. The Giants won 45-38, but I felt like I'd lost a friend.

27

A week after the Super Bowl, I was in my dorm room packing my bag. The ancient furnace was rumbling as always. The old wood spoke of legacy, but my thoughts were in the future. I tied my shoes, put on my overcoat, and walked out.

My driver was holding the sedan's back door open for me. I stepped in, and then his black gloves took the steering wheel like a man holds his wife. We drove in silence through the early dawn mist. The Massachusetts hills were green and wet. In one of my classes I'd been learning how, not long ago, blankets of snow covered this area most of the winter. There had not been a single flake since my freshman year.

We pulled up to the private airport where I boarded my family's jet. I'd asked my dad about it during our monthly video chat. He'd smiled one of his rare, intrigued smiles and asked me, *So you like this girl?* I told him yes and began to say more, but a business call had pulled him away—same as always. At least I had the plane and its pilot.

I finished a tomato juice, an egg sandwich, and a few minutes of reading for class by the time we landed in North Carolina. The sky was clear and blue. It was warm enough to take off my coat. No wonder most of the country lived in southern cities. Only DC was important enough to justify a shield and its warming side effects.

I got into another black sedan that was waiting for me. This airport was within the auto-grid, so the car needed no driver. It moved with mechanical precision, but there was not the same rhythm as when a black-gloved maestro manned the wheel.

The car turned off a highway and into a neighborhood of little brick houses. They were all the same, with one story and black shutters. I figured the neighborhood had looked just like this when they built it a hundred years ago, except for the solar panels gleaming on their roofs.

After a few identical streets, the car came to a stop in front of one of the nondescript homes. I swiped my wrist to pay and stepped out.

The house's plain black door swung open an instant later. Naomi stood in the doorway, looking like a goddess descended to the pits of suburbia.

"Welcome to Durham!" she said.

"Thanks!" I moved toward her, or maybe she pulled me closer. "It's good to be here."

She grabbed my hand and tugged me into the house,

sparing me of having to decide whether to hug her.

"Daddy and I spend a lot of time in DC, but this is our home." She gestured to the tiny space as if it were a mansion's parlor. Three old couches ringed the room and dozens of books were scattered around the floor. "Come on." She dragged me further inside. "I convinced everyone to take a walk, so it's all ours for now."

The tour of the house took maybe three minutes. There was a kitchen, four bedrooms, and that was pretty much it. Three of the bedrooms had bunks. None of the rooms were as big as my bathroom in our Manhattan apartment.

The tour stopped in a tiny bedroom. "This is my room." Naomi pointed to a desk in the corner. There were three holographic screens and a precept-syncing station. It was like mine, only an older model. "This is where I do my work, and where I talk to you. Notice anything different compared to the rest of the house?"

"You live in the twenty-first century?"

"Exactly!" she replied. "Daddy noticed early on that I liked technology, so even though he gives away most of his money, he has always gotten me the best and the newest stuff, as long as it pushed me to be better. *You gotta follow your calling,*" she said, copying the low voice of her father.

She made me smile, a real smile. Something about her forced the rest of the world to disappear behind me. The sound of a door opening interrupted us, but she stepped closer to me. "Let's go meet my family," she whispered.

I put my hand on her cheek and kissed her. Just another peck, but nothing about a sync, no matter how good, could compare to real touch.

She smiled at me. "I was kind of hoping you'd do that."

She led me into the living room with the three couches. I knew she had a big family, but seeing them standing there was surprising all the same. Her dad was beside her four younger brothers and her older sister.

"Welcome to our home," her father said. "I'm not sure if you remember, but I'm Moses. We met before." He held out his giant hand, which swallowed mine in a firm shake.

"Of course. It is good to see you again." Did he really think I could forget him?

"This is Rachel." He stepped back and she stepped forward. She was taller than Naomi, almost as tall as Moses.

"I've heard a lot about you," said Rachel, looking me up and down. "I watch over this brood while Daddy and Naomi are off on their travels. Nothing happens in this house without my knowing it."

"What kind of surveillance?" I asked.

The boys started laughing as if I'd said the funniest thing in the world.

"Not funny," she said, turning to her brothers. Their lips shut and their backs straightened. A look of satisfaction was on her face when she turned to me again. "I don't need cameras or microphones, Elijah. The Lord guides my vision and whispers the truth in my ears."

"Well," I started to say something smart back, but Naomi stopped me with a light elbow to my side. Instead I said, "Nice to meet you, Rachel."

She nodded. "Boys?"

"I'm Abraham," said the oldest of them. He was a lanky teenage version of his dad.

"Isaac," said the next one. He barely looked like the others, with his straight blond hair and blue eyes.

"We're Jacob and Joseph!" announced the youngest ones together. They were twins who looked about ten years old and full of trouble.

"So that's my family," said Naomi. "We'll head out for dinner soon, but maybe we could hang out here for a while?" She dipped her head slightly, adorably.

I nodded.

Next thing I knew, we were all sitting in the living room playing some board game. I had no idea what was going on, but they talked and laughed as if this was the greatest day they'd had on earth.

Somewhere along the way, Naomi's sister Rachel mentioned their mom. Moses went quiet then. But after the game was over, he brought her up again.

"You've met us now," he said, "but to really know us you have to learn about their mother. She was the most beautiful woman to grace the earth. How else do you think they got their looks?" He motioned to his children, whose faint smiles did little to hide the suddenly somber mood in the room. "Naomi?" he asked.

"Yes, Daddy." She stepped to the front of the room and pressed her wrist. A life-sized holograph sprang to life before us. It was a pretty blonde woman.

My jaw dropped open. I knew her. She was the woman from my dream, the woman who was on the white side, talking to the man on the black side. I remembered her words clearly—*You must protect her.*

"What?" Naomi asked me.

"Oh, it's just—" I hesitated. "It's just that she almost looks familiar, probably because she looks so much like you."

"That's what I've always said," rumbled Moses's voice.

Four little kids ran into the image, two girls and two boys. The mother swooped down and wrapped her arms around them. Then she stood and faced us.

"Number five on the way," she said, patting her small round belly. I figured the recording was from Moses's precept, from what he'd seen, because this woman with Naomi's green eyes was looking at us with affectionate, beaming joy. Then the holograph faded.

"Turns out number five was also number six," Naomi explained. "Twins."

"Is she—" I fumbled for words to ask what had happened to her. In my dream she had been as real as Naomi beside me.

"She died giving birth," Rachel said. Her expression was flat.

"Every day with her was a blessing." Moses stood, and so did the rest of us. "But we all make sacrifices. Whether we know it or not, every second is an opportunity to give ourselves up for others." He suddenly clapped his hands. "No long faces, now. What would your mother say?"

"*The joy of the Lord is your strength!*" the boys shouted.

"That He is." Moses smiled. "We've got a little while

before dark. Why don't we get in a game of hoops, so these two can have their dinner?"

The four boys were already sprinting out the door, with Moses and Rachel following after them.

28

"Why did my mom look familiar?" Naomi asked. "I saw it in your face. You recognized her."

I studied the organic peas on my plate. I prodded them with my fork, as if I could avoid her question, as if I could get through dinner without telling her about my dream.

I looked up. Naomi wore a knowing smile.

"I told you," I said. "She has your exact eyes."

"And? What are you hiding?"

"You win," I confessed, "no longer will I hide that your beauty has conquered me. How is your steak?"

"Exquisite." Her lean fingers guided her knife and fork to slice the red meat. She took a bite slowly, keeping her eyes on mine. She chewed, taunting me with her patience, as if she knew she would get her answer. She swallowed. "It's funny that I've lived so close to this place and never eaten here. Too expensive, I guess. Want to try mine?"

I nodded. She sliced off another piece and reached over the table with her fork. I looked down the length of her perfect, bare arm as I took the bite. It was delicious.

"Do you always order steak?" I asked.

"Daddy is vegan, so I seize my chances."

"Rebel," I said, and she grinned.

The bubbly waitress stepped up to our table. "How is everything, Mr. Goldsmith?"

"Quite good. Thanks."

She placed a glass of red wine in front of me, then put her hand on my shoulder. Her fingernails were bright pink against my black velvet blazer. It struck me that Naomi would never paint her nails—reason number eighty-three that I liked her. "Our sommelier insists you try this pairing," the waitress said. "It's on us, of course."

I swirled the wine and sniffed it. "Peppercorn, radish, and leather." Naomi laughed under her breath. I took a sip. "Delicious," I told the waitress. "I'll have to tell my father about it."

"Oh, that would be excellent." She clasped her hands. "Please, enjoy, and do not hesitate to flag me if you need anything, anything at all." She bowed lightly and slipped away.

"Is there anything your dad doesn't own?" Naomi asked.

"Lots of things, but he got interested in these classic restaurants a few years back. He always says, *Service never goes out of style.* So he invested in places like this. You can't see an ounce of technology in here."

"It's really nice. I like the candles."

"Me too. They make your face glow." I took another sip of the wine and then held the glass toward her. "Want to try? It is fantastic with the steak—like paradise in your mouth, with notes of black currant. I was kidding about the radish."

"I figured that out, but no, thank you. I'm pretty sure paradise can't fit in my mouth. Buy your tickets yet?"

"I bought both of our tickets. First class on a luxury airline, arriving early on Friday, April 9."

Her eyes grew wide. "You bought my ticket? First class?"

"My dad has a business trip that week, so our jet is not available. First class is the next best option."

"I guess so." She slumped her shoulders in mock disappointment. If I was to have any chance of keeping Charles's warning in mind, I needed to keep my eyes off her shoulders. "Thank you," she smiled. "It is going to be an amazing trip. But you can't buy your way out of answering my question." She cut off a large piece of meat.

"Which question?"

"My mother, tell me how you recognized her." She took the bite and sat back, waiting.

"A dream," I began. "She was in my dream. This one was different. Your mom and some other guy dressed in black were talking to me. She told me I had to go, but she didn't say where. He told me I couldn't go. That's all."

"*That's all?*" she chided. "You're still a bad liar. When's your next ISA-7 exam?"

"July, why?"

"Good, there's still time to practice." She laughed. I didn't think it was funny. "You know you're going to have to tell me more about the dream."

"That depends," I said.

"On what?"

"On what you'll tell me."

"Oh, you have questions for me?" she mused. "Go ahead and ask."

I could not hold back a smile. No one talked to me like her. "Have you had any missions yet?"

"You know the answer to that," she said. "You always know where I am, and we've talked pretty regularly."

"Nice try. I know only where your body is, not your mind." With Charles gone from school almost all the time, I figured Naomi had to have gone on missions as well. "Aren't Christians supposed to tell the truth?"

For an instant her calm lifted and a touch of red blushed across her cheeks. "You know I can't tell you," she said. "Please don't ask."

"Okay. Just for tonight, no more questions about ISA-7, and no more questions about my dreams. Fair enough?"

"Maybe, if you agree to talk to Bart again. Just one more time before our trip."

"Seriously?"

She nodded. "These dreams could be very important. At the least, you owe it to yourself to learn about them."

"Fine, I'll talk to Bart." If anything, talking to him might make me feel normal, compared to his crazy ideas. "So we'll leave these questions alone until after our trip. And maybe in Italy we'll try a real kiss. Sound good?"

"Always pushing, aren't you?" Her grin was smooth, but thanks to our sync, I knew her heart was racing, her blood pressure rising.

"Yeah." I didn't need to say more. She knew my heart rate, too.

"I'll think about it." Her playfulness was suddenly gone. "It would help a lot if you started to believe."

"Believe what? I thought your order picked me as some sort of chosen one." I pointed to myself for emphasis. "Isn't that enough?"

"How about believe in God, for starters?"

"Consider that box checked. Remember, I'm Jewish."

"By birth," she tested. "I'm not so sure by faith."

I flashed her my best smile, unwilling to admit she was right. As far as the faithful went, I was at the bottom of the ladder. "I believe in love," I said, "and you say God is love, so there."

She nodded. "It's a start. God is love and much more." She leaned forward, beaming like a lighthouse. "Elijah, you are holding yourself back. You would see more if you had faith, and I believe the world *needs* you to see more."

"Why? What does the world need me to see?"

"Your dreams and more, much more. Weren't you listening to Bart?"

"We agreed not to talk about my dreams." I felt like I was plugging a dam that was about to break. We'd have to overcome this faith thing eventually, but I didn't want to spoil our night. "I'd rather talk about us," I said. "I like you, Naomi. A lot. And you like me, too."

A conflicted look passed over her face. Too bad the sync couldn't tell me her thoughts. Her face went smooth again. After an eternal moment of hesitation, she nodded. Her heart was pounding. "Yes, I like you, Elijah."

"So what's holding you back?"

"I'm not holding back," she said. "I would hardly sync with a boy I didn't like, much less kiss him. What else could you want from me?"

"Honesty." The word flew from my lips like a caged bird set free. "What are you and your order up to?"

"You know better than any of us, because you've seen it. We are serving the Lord." She suddenly smiled. "But no more talk of dreams, right? Let's just assume I'm letting you court me because it's useful cover. You get my affection, and I get to take you on my mission to Rome. But there's one condition."

So it was a *mission*—now I just needed to figure it out. "There's always a condition," I said. "What is it?"

"You have to *try* to believe. Be serious about it. I fear the stakes are higher than either of us know."

I pushed away my nagging doubts and the warning bells. Opportunities like this—the heart-pounding, face-flushing kind—were not to be missed. "So if I agree to try," I said, "I can make you fall crazy in love with me?"

She laughed. "You can try."

I nodded. "Good. So I'll give it a try, and we'll see where that leads."

The rest of the evening passed in an excited blur. We talked of food, books, and Italy. Nothing about it made me nervous. If anything, it just made me nervous about Charles. Naomi seemed to be the normal one.

We rode back to Naomi's house and parted on her doorstep. She wouldn't risk a kiss with her family in the house. I was still just an ISA friend to them. As I flew back to the gothic campus in Massachusetts, the night felt bland and cold in comparison. But there was a bright spark in the night, a pulse in my mind—the beating heart of Naomi. I was not going to lose that pulse.

29

"We could have had this conversation virtually," I said to Bart. This time it was just the two of us in his little office. For some reason, it seemed more comfortable that way. I did not have to behave for Naomi, but I would hold up my part of the deal and *try* to believe. Good thing we never said how hard I had to try.

"Technology is a cover up." The large priest stroked his grey goatee. "It makes the world faster, more efficient, more open, but better? In some ways, yes, but it obscures what matters most: the soul. Anyone can play god with a nanochip in the head. You spend enough time playing god and then you forget that there's a real God up there."

"Fine," I replied. "No technology. I'm already here." Bart's diatribe reminded me to keep my mouth shut. Everything would go smoother that way. "You've got an hour," I said. "I'm listening."

Bart shook his heavy head gravely. "Such a pittance for the weighty things on your mind." He stood and stepped to the bookshelf covering one side of the room. "Tea?"

"Sure. Thanks."

An old water heater was plugged into the wall. He poured steaming liquid into two small, porcelain cups. His fat finger barely fit through the quarter-sized handle.

"I was in Morocco last week and brought back this tea," he explained. "They know how to make a fine tea."

"You travel?" I sipped the tea. It was hot and good. Why on earth had this man gone to Morocco? I decided not to ask that, or if he traveled by boat.

He lumbered back to the chair behind his desk. It squeaked when he sat, as if in protest. "I travel a lot." He smelled his tea and took a sip. "My order is an international one, with many ties around the world."

"Your order?" I feigned ignorance, hoping to pry into what I needed to learn.

"I mentioned it before," he said. "It's called the Order of John."

"A secret order?"

His sudden grin hinted at intrigue, or maybe it was just the flickering candlelight. "Are you ready to learn more?"

I nodded and tried to get comfortable in the hard chair.

"Last time," he began, "I told you about John, the apostle, on Patmos. Well, like most of us, John died. In the generations after his death, his band of closest followers formed into a secret group of twelve living men. These men are the Order of John. The order first embedded itself in the Catholic Church and in other halls of power. No one knew its members except the members themselves. They carried the legacy of John and the keys to the Book of Revelation. Many called the book heresy. They called it crazy. They said it did not belong in the Bible. But our order made sure it remained, an odd but fitting conclusion to history's best-selling book."

So far Bart was making sense to me—a crazy group of men were responsible for a crazy ending to the Bible. I could go along with that. "Why did others not want the Bible to end with this revelation book?"

"Read it some time," he encouraged. "You'll learn about beasts, destruction, a seven-headed dragon, and locusts with hair like a woman, teeth like a lion, and breastplates of iron."

I had to laugh a little at that. "Armored insects?"

"Exactly," Bart said, "so you see why the book's been controversial? Well, my order has long known that many of these details were fulfilled in the Romans' destruction of Jerusalem in 70 AD. Let me give you an example. Ever heard of the number 666?"

I nodded. "You Christians say it's an evil number."

"Yes, but John had something specific in mind. He wrote the number as a code to his fellow believers. He said, *Let him who has understanding calculate the number of the beast, for it is the number of a man: His number is 666.* Well, the Caesar at the time was Nero. In Hebrew his name was *Nrwn Osr.* The numeric value of those seven Hebrew letters is 50, 200, 6, 50, 100, 60, and 200—totaling 666. The book of Revelation was a letter to John's friends, and the Hebrew was a code they could understand but the Romans could not. The letter was a warning that Rome would destroy Jerusalem, and so it did a few years after John's vision."

"Okay," I said, not admitting that Bart's explanation made a lot more sense than what I'd found through a standard precept search about Christians and the end of the world. "So John saw it coming. But it still happened, and history marched on. Why are we still talking about it?"

"Because that does not explain the last three chapters of the book. Ever heard of the thousand years, the millennium?"

"For one of my classes, I read some funny stuff about people who thought the world was going to end in 2000. Looks like they were wrong."

"Many have been wrong about when the world will end. Not everyone has your vision, Elijah. I believe the era of wrong guesses will soon be over."

I would take his bait, especially if it would get us out of first-century history. "Why, and when?" I asked.

"The priceless questions," Bart said. "Even within the order there is disagreement. Some think the thousand years is a symbolic number, meaning just a long time until the Messiah comes again. That's what Augustine and Luther thought. They may be right."

"Who are Augustine and Luther?"

Bart looked at me with surprise. "Nevermind that for now. Here's my best guess. John was right about the thousand years, only it took two millennia to get there.

1066 AD holds the key."

"The year 1066?" I asked, confused.

He nodded. "In the 1060s, the Duke of Normandy, now known as William the Conqueror, visited the pope before invading Britain. The Duke was a strong man with an open mind. The pope knew this and used it. You see, this pope was also a member of our order. He believed that William's voyage to conquer England was part of a divine plan. The pope blessed William and his conquest. With that blessing, William sailed his army to Britain. When he first set foot on the ground, he stumbled and fell to his knees. He grabbed the sand in his fists and held it up for his men. 'Look, I have already grasped my Kingdom.' Those words came to be. The conqueror got a fifth of all the country's land. But it was more than that. We believe William's kingdom served the kingdom of God. His reign over England was no mere shift in the provinces of man. It was a landmark in history's passage because it heralded the binding of the dragon for *another* thousand years."

I had been nodding here and there as Bart spoke. I had tried, as I'd promised Naomi, to pay attention. But Bart was sounding crazy again. Now he was staring at me, wide-eyed. "Thanks for the history lesson," I said. "You want to tell me why any of this is relevant?"

"That is exactly what I want to tell you," he replied. "The dragon, the one *you* have seen, is more than a creature. It is a concept, too. It is chaos and destruction, not by nature, but by man. It is Satan unleashed *through* man. Man at its worst. Man as animal. The dragon brings war and death and misery. I believe that John foresaw the dragon's bindings undone in 1066—a thousand years from when he had the vision. But I think the world wasn't ready. The fall would have been too soft. There were so few people. They were so disconnected. Now the world is ready. Another thousand years have passed. The limits of society, and constraints of law, they will be unbound. The dragon will be unbound. Terror will reign, the world will end, and you will be there to watch it."

He was silent then, waiting again for me to answer.

"That's dark stuff, man." I'd rather not believe a word of it, but it sounded a lot more reasonable if the dragon was symbolic instead of a literal creature. "Why are you telling me all this?"

"We need your vision. You can see what others cannot, but you have to believe. Naomi needs you to believe."

"Why? You expect me to believe your theories?"

"Not fully," he admitted. "I told you, none of us know all the answers. But you should trust in the gifts God has given to you."

"You call my dreams *gifts*?"

"Oh yes, Elijah." He nodded slowly. "They are gifts to you, for the sake of the world."

"I think the world's going to keep on spinning."

Bart sighed, as if I'd said something profound. "Many think the same thing. Even a few in my order. Call me crazy, but I've seen what you've seen. He *will* be unbound."

"You've had the dreams, too?" I had to admit, that would be interesting.

"Yes." He shivered slightly. "It has been many years. I saw hints of a dragon and a man. I saw hints of what you saw, but I lack your gift of sight. The only thing my dreams showed clearly was you...coming to me."

"You saw me? How do you know?"

"Because I saw your face, Elijah. And you're a Jewish son from the Roeh line. A brilliant girl brought this boy to me, this boy with dreams. I could be wrong about the timing, the thousand years, and everything else. But I'm *not* wrong about you."

"So what's it supposed to mean, your dreams?"

"They mean I believe in *you*," Bart said, like a declaration of faith. "I believe you are chosen, you are gifted, you are the one who can see."

"Why me?" His conviction stirred something deep down. No one had ever said something like that to me.

"I wish I knew, Elijah. I wish I knew about Naomi, too. I'm pretty sure I'll have to enter heaven before I know the Lord's reasons. We're just guessing at the shadows with our feeble brains."

I let his words sink in. "So let's assume for a second that you're right. What am I supposed to see? And what does Naomi have to do with this?"

"I cannot tell a seer what he will see." He pointed at me. "That is your task. You must stay with Naomi to be her eyes, her protector."

He sounded a lot like Naomi's mother in my dreams. Maybe he could answer my biggest question: "Protect her from what?"

"When *he* is unleashed, *he* will seek her."

"Abaddon? Why?"

Bart shrugged. "I've said most of what I know. You can know more than anyone, if you will believe."

"I am trying," I said.

"Try harder, because *he* knows your role, and he will seek to corrupt it, just as he will seek to corrupt her. You are running out of time."

"Can't you tell me more?" I tried to tell myself that I was asking because I didn't want to come back to Bart again. No way should I actually want to know his theories. But now I was a bit curious.

He shook his head. "We've reached the limits of my guidance. I dare not speak things that are not truth. You must find it out yourself. You must believe, Elijah."

I left his office feeling more confused than ever. Part of me wanted him to be right. What if I really was unique, chosen? But part of me refused to believe it. This man, holed up in a dungeon with candles, had just told me he dreamed about me! It was too weird—almost as weird as a dragon being unleashed and the world ending this year, and I most certainly did not believe that.

When I woke in my bed at school the next morning, the word *believe* was ringing in my ears. I could not shake Bart's words. They hung over my mind like a cloud. Had Bart really just been talking to me, or was he trying to manipulate me as part of some bigger plot? Could this have something to do with ISA?

Charles's warning sprang to mind again.

I wondered how much Naomi knew, and how much she was hiding. Her steady heartbeat was hundreds of miles away.

30

It was March 26, about a week after I'd met with Bart. His words and warnings seemed distant on this perfect early spring day. It was the kind of day that crashes the hardest when you learn someone died.

It was after calculus class. I was sitting on an old stone bench outside. The sky was blue and the sun warmed the world. My pale skin drank it in while the birds sang. The bright green blades of flowers sliced up through the earth, ready any moment to flower, to explode into color.

Then I made a bad decision. I summoned V's briefing screens. They obscured the bright green grass and trees behind them. The center screen showed Naomi's video message. "Elijah," she said, her eyes puffy and red. Her voice caught, then she continued in a whisper, "We lost Charles."

No. That was impossible. I had glimpsed him just

yesterday, walking to class.

"You'll want to know how," she continued. "And you know I can't tell you. It was on a mission. That's all I can say."

I figured she would stop then, maybe cry. But instead her somber gaze gripped me like a vice while she spoke on.

"I'm so sorry, Elijah. I wish I could be there with you, but I cannot talk to you about this, and I will be away a couple weeks on duty. You will understand in time."

I doubted that. She would say nothing of her missions. Charles's death only gave me more doubts about her and the trip to Rome.

"Stay strong," she said, as if reading my mind across time and space. "Two more weeks, and I'll be sitting beside you on a plane heading to Rome." Her eyes were moist as she blew me a kiss. The message was over.

I turned off the screens without checking any other messages. The sun was still shining, the birds still singing. The grass was still green. But now Charles was dead.

I sat there in silence until my next class. I didn't know what else to do. I stumbled through the day and ate dinner alone, in disbelief. I tried reaching Naomi, Aisha, Wade, and even Patrick. No one responded. I skipped my studies and went straight to sleep.

By the next morning, everyone in school had heard the news. The guys were all talking about it in the halls. *How did he die? He was in class just yesterday. You know he was picked to be a fellow in that government agency? The International Security Agency? Yeah, that one. I bet he was a spy. I bet the Chinese killed him. Maybe he bit one of those poison pills, the kind spies keep in their mouths to make sure no torture makes them spill their secrets. Is that suicide, then? No, it's government service, the highest kind. Charles is a hero. An American hero.*

And so the rumors spread.

Eventually I turned on my earphones. I searched for songs with violins and a swooning voice. V knew what I wanted better than I did. She found a playlist of five songs. I listened to those same five, over and over, until the eulogy for Charles the next day. I had been chosen to speak.

When the service came, a few hundred students gathered in the chapel. The perfect spring weather held outside. Sunlight streamed through the arched, stained glass windows. It made my classmates look brilliant, glittering in red and blue and yellow.

I walked to the podium as if in a trance. So many eyes were on me. V reduced my focus, so I wouldn't have to look at anyone in particular. Then she enhanced my vocal chords. At least her presence in my life was reliable.

"Charles was a nerd," I began. I heard a few gasps, as I'd expected. I wasn't here to sugarcoat things. Charles would not have wanted that. "He was the first one to teach me how to hack into others' precepts, five years ago, before the government had to change the whole precept system because of him. He probably taught some of you how to configure glasses so that the teachers wouldn't catch you watching movies in class. He always wore his glasses. Sometimes I wonder if he saw a brighter world through them. He laughed a lot, Charles did. He made me laugh, too. I bet everyone in this room who ever talked to Charles has laughed with Charles."

Many heads in the room nodded. I pressed on.

"A nerd, you see, never takes himself too seriously. He invites others into his world, as long as they are willing to leave their pride at the door. A nerd is a genius, a pioneer of some sort. A great nerd, one like Charles, makes the systems of the world bend around him because of his brilliance. Some systems of man will never bend, though. Systems like war and terror and power. They don't give for nerds. They swallow them up and use them for their purposes. So what was a guy like Charles to do? He could let the powers swallow him, or he could punch them in the face. I'm sure that's what Charles did. We may never know the truth, but I bet he punched a giant dragon. That's how we should remember him."

I took two swings at the air, fake punches, the way Charles used to do. I saw a few pained smiles in the crowd.

"Maybe he paid with his life, but he showed us what courage is. A nerd with courage. If we all followed that lead, Charles would be alive, watching movies, laughing. Instead he's dead. Honor him. Don't let the powers swallow you."

I stopped and the chapel was deathly silent. I had prepared a speech in my head and it included almost none of the words that had left my mouth. I walked back to my seat and sat down. I wiped the sweat from my brow and the tears from my eyes. My hands were shaking.

They stopped shaking that night, when I got the

message from Patrick. I was sitting alone in my dorm room. The message sprang into my mind, designated urgent, with an override of anything else. It was one of those top-secret notes that blinks on your screen for half a minute and then disappears forever.

I'm sorry, man. I was with Charles when he died. We were on a mission in late January. His death came fast. It was painless. Just before we lost him, he gave me a message for you. He said you should trust Naomi. I don't know why he said that. None of it makes sense anymore. Good luck. Your friend, P.

That was it. The letters vanished just as I finished reading them the third time.

It would have been hard enough to believe the words if they had stayed fixed on my screen. With them gone, though, doubts raged like wildfire.

Somebody was lying. Something was wrong. Very wrong.

I'd seen Charles many times since late January. I'd even sat beside him at the Super Bowl. He was living and breathing then. He'd said the exact opposite of Patrick's message, that I should *not* trust Naomi. Did Patrick really have the guts to make up something like that? Why would he? Maybe I didn't like the guy much, but he had always been honest.

V walked me through my memories. Charles had seemed off ever since we'd finished our week at ISA-7. Even at the Super Bowl, he'd looked sick. He'd snapped at me, for the first time ever, about not going to Rome. He hadn't been himself.

The words of Sven, the ISA techie, suddenly came to me. *But we can reconstruct a fresh corpse. You can occupy it.*

I fell back into my bed. I closed my eyes, and the room and the world began to spin around me.

31

"I heard about your friend." My dad had his back to me. He looked out a wall of glass over the towering skyscrapers of Manhattan. The green and metallic vertical lines of the city matched his pinstripes. He had shut down his precept. It was a bad sign, especially since he rarely called for me like this.

"What did you hear?" I sat in one of the deep leather chairs facing his desk. No one had desks like his anymore. It must have taken a whole redwood to build the thing.

"You gave a speech to your classmates." He turned to me. A glass of scotch was in his hand. This was his second already since I'd been in his office.

"Yes sir." I met his stare. Today would be different. I was not going to let him intimidate me.

"It seems you caused quite a stir." He walked around the desk and leaned back against it, swirling his drink. The ice cubes clinked against the crystal.

"I don't know about that."

"The dean of Princeton, Garret Blythe, is a friend of mine. He called me." He took a sip. "He's worried about you, son, and so am I."

"Why?"

"Isn't that obvious?"

"No," I lied. The past months had been a thunderstorm—Naomi was the lightening, Charles the thunder, and my dreams the black clouds. "I'm still enrolling this fall."

"Of course you are." My dad smiled, the way he always did before he demanded something of me. "That's why I want you to take it easy before your first semester. You graduate in a little over a month, yes?"

"That's right, the third Saturday of May."

"I will be there." He finished his scotch and sat in the other leather chair across from me. His hands gripped the chair's arms firmly. "Listen, Elijah, I know this is hard."

He had no idea.

"I am trying to protect you, son."

"I know." But I didn't.

"Good." He paused. "I want you to drop this ISA business."

"What?"

"You have noble intentions, I can see that."

"This isn't about being noble. Our country needs people like me to serve."

"You failed the test."

"I will take it again this summer."

"No, you won't."

I rose to my feet, and so did he.

"This is not an argument," he said.

"No," my voice rose, "because you can't stop me."

"I already have," he replied.

"What do you mean?"

"Sit down." I stayed on my feet. "Please, sit, let me explain, and then we can discuss."

He sat, and I reluctantly did the same.

"I won't lose you like I lost your mother." He looked away, toward the window. He hadn't mentioned her in years. "I spoke with the ISA Director in Geneva, Beatriz Silva. We agreed it was best if you postponed your enrollment a while. Finish your first year at Princeton. If you still want to enlist, then I won't stand in your way. You'll have to pass the test, of course."

"You promise not to interfere again?"

The faintest wince crossed over his face.

"What did you do?" I asked. "Rig the first test?"

"No." He shook his head. "I promise. But I was consulted when they learned about your dreams. They asked me strange questions, son. They asked me if you had any reason to dream of strange images, things like dragons and destroyed cities. I told them the truth, that you didn't. What's going on in there?" He pointed at my forehead. "I'm worried about you."

I stood and walked to the window behind his desk. The sun had dipped halfway into the Hudson River. The lights of a thousand buildings began to shine against the coming darkness. It was my favorite time of day. The view calmed my nerves.

"I'm fine, dad," I eventually said.

He had stepped to my side, and at my words, he put his arm over my shoulders. We both looked out together. It was easier than looking at each other. "That's what I've said for years about losing your mother."

"I thought you were telling the truth."

"Sometimes I did, too."

"You have to let me try the test again."

"I will, but not now. I can't bear to lose you. You've had these visions, you've lost a friend, and this girl is distracting you."

"Why shouldn't she distract me?" I turned to look at him, defiance creeping into my stance.

He looked at me calmly, too calmly. "When the Director called me in January, she asked about Naomi as well. The girl was in your visions, and she was in your class. I learned that you two synced. You've been spending a lot of time with her. I saw the charges. A night at the Inn at Little Washington, a trip to North Carolina, and you plan to go to Rome in a week. You're young, and this is moving awfully fast. When were you going to talk to me about her?"

"I already told you the basics, last time we talked. You cut our monthly chat short. You've been busy."

"I make time for you when you need me."

"Is that a joke? What makes you think I need you?"

His gaze hardened, then softened again. "Don't try to live your life alone, son. You can do it, but it hurts."

"I've seen that." An emotion gripped me, something like sympathy. "That's why you have to let me take the test. Naomi is already in."

"Isn't it enough that I let you date her?"

"What is that supposed to mean?"

"She and her family, they're not like us."

"You mean they love each other?" I regretted the words as they left my mouth.

"They're many things we're not. Like *Christians*, for starters, and not the mainstream kind." His voice was full of disgust and contempt. "You get my point?"

"They're real people, good people. And she's more beautiful every time I see her. Isn't that what you always said about mom?"

"Yes." He pressed his eyes closed. "But she was even more beautiful inside. She had the most amazing faith, the most amazing dreams." His eyes blinked open. "What about your faith, son? What do you think she would say about this?"

"What about it? She's been gone ten years. It doesn't matter anymore. Are you going to tell me now that you believe in God?"

He looked away, out the window, and was quiet. I took that as a no—I figured his only gods lived in the dollar and the bottom of an empty glass. But then something he said hit me. My mom had dreams? He'd never mentioned that before.

"What kind of dreams did mom have?" I asked.

"I don't want to talk about it." He sounded hurt. "They were just dreams. Vivid dreams about things that it seems were not to be."

"Like what?"

He turned to me with a curious gaze. "She dreamed you were something special, son. She told me her dreams were like shadows of what you would see."

Shadows. That reminded me of Bart's words.

"Does that mean you once believed in her dreams?"

He nodded. "I once did," he said, "before they found the growth in her brain. You know what they said, it affected her thinking those last years...until we lost her."

His head sagged, and I went to him. We embraced each other for the first time in years, and we were silent then, silent for a long time. Was he right about mom and the growth? Or was she right? I realized my dad was not the one to ask.

"I'm sorry," I said as we released each other. "You're right, this has been a tough stretch. I'll hold off on the ISA test if you stay out of my relationship with Naomi, okay?"

When he turned to me, he looked like he understood. "Okay," he nodded, "better to love and hurt than to never love at all. Enjoy Rome. I'll see you at graduation."

*　　　*　　　*

That night, after talking to my dad, I had V search my database of memories for anything about my mom and dreams. She found one match. It was from April 2051, during Passover. It was the year they'd found the abnormal growth, five years before my mom died. I was almost three years old. I'd watched the memory many times, but I hadn't revisited it in years. I'd forgotten what it had to do with dreams.

I closed my eyes and asked V to play the memory.

Suddenly I was in the modest home of my mom's parents in Jerusalem. A bright blue toy truck was in my pudgy hand. I pushed it along the old wooden floors, making zooming sounds as I went.

The truck's path led around the room where my parents were staying. The smell was so familiar. It was my mom's fragrance of oil and citrus and sweet spices. Over the zooming noise from my mouth, I could hear her and dad talking. I could not see them, with my gaze locked on the truck, but the toddler-me *felt* secure in the memory.

"Rabbi Zachariah will be there," my dad was saying.

"Who better to preside over the Seder?" Was that a hint of irony in my mother's voice? "He's one I will not miss after we return home."

My almost three-year-old mind must have understood the word "home," because the memory's view swung to my parents. My mother was standing in front of a mirror and wearing a beautiful black dress. My dad stood close behind her, rubbing her shoulders. They smiled at each other through the mirror. The scene ripped at me, chewed me inside. No wonder I avoided memories like these.

"Zachariah is just an old man," my dad said, as my view returned to the truck and the floor. "Wouldn't you be curious about someone with dreams like your recent ones?"

"I should never have mentioned them," my mom said dismissively.

"But you believe they're important," replied my dad, in a tone suggesting he did not quite share that belief. It reminded me of the tone I'd used with Naomi about her faith.

"We agreed not to talk about it anymore," my mom sighed. "No one knows what the dreams mean. My family, the Roeh from Samuel on down, we've long had visions. We keep saying Israel is hardening, but the gifts and the calling of God are irrevocable."

"And your dreams say Elijah has the gift. That's why you picked the name, right?"

My little face had turned up to them again upon hearing my name. I rolled my truck to them and reached my short arms as far as I could to hold onto both their legs.

"We agreed not to talk about it," my mom repeated, as she swept me up in her arms. Her touch and smell were paradise. Her dark eyes looked deep into mine. "My little man will chart his own path someday. He is a Roeh as well as a Goldsmith, so his vision will guide him." She tapped my nose playfully, and I laughed.

She glanced to my dad. "But let's not contaminate his innocent mind. His precept is recording all this. He'll have clearer memories than we ever could. So remember," she spoke to me, "trust what God reveals to you, no matter what. Okay, Elijah?"

"No!" toddler-me proclaimed in response, obviously not understanding what she meant. My parents both burst out in laughter and pressed me between them in a hug.

V stopped the video. There were no more records of my mom mentioning dreams. Good thing, too. I could not bear to see her and my dad like that, happy and together.

I wondered whether my dad was right about loving and hurting. Was it really better? I resolved to test it, and to test my dreams, to see whether there was any truth to them. I would be Naomi however I could—even on a plane to Rome.

32

Seat 2A was the best on the jet, because Naomi was in 2B. I'd offered her the window, but she had declined. My right arm was on the armrest between us, and her hand was on mine. I loved the feel of her fingers. Her grip was assuring, holding me in the present, keeping the past and future at bay.

"We can watch any movie we want?" She flipped through the options on the screen before her. We'd lifted off just a few minutes ago.

"Anything ever made," I said. "That's how it works in first class. We could probably watch three movies before this flight is over. These commercial jets are more comfortable than they used to be, but hardly any faster. It's too bad my dad's jet wasn't available. Then we'd be in Rome in a couple hours." Not that I was in a hurry for Naomi to move her hand. I put my other hand on hers.

She kept her eyes on the different movie titles scrolling in front of her. She pulled her long legs up onto the seat and crossed them. Her knees bounced up and down lightly, like she was an excited little girl. I leaned over her shoulder and watched the screen with her.

"How about something older?" she asked, turning to me. "I'd love to watch a classic."

"How old?"

"I don't know, something *really* old, like before digital manipulation."

V helped me sort through every classic in my mind, searching for a perfect mood-setter. Not too happy, not too dark. Not too sappy, but romantic, artistic, with a great score. Maybe something set in Europe. Then it hit me.

"Have you ever seen *Amelie*?" I asked.

She shook her head. "You know I didn't watch many movies growing up. I've never heard of that one."

"It's definitely a classic. Filmed at the end of the last century and set in Paris. The soundtrack is a thing of legend. I study to it sometimes. It's beautiful."

"*Amelie* it is." She leaned close to me, putting her forehead against mine. "Everything I get through our sync makes me more intrigued. I'd love to see and hear what's beautiful to you."

We each entered the selection into the plane's system, and seconds later the movie was rolling. The opening song danced into my ears, taking me away with Naomi to a simpler time. She squeezed my hand, tight.

Our attendant served dinner while we watched the

movie. It was a delicious wild salmon, rare these days. I had a glass of white wine. Naomi had water. Amelie went on her adventures through Paris, secretly helping others in her charming way. The piano and accordions made her movements look almost as graceful as Naomi's. By the time the credits scrolled, I felt a million miles away from the recent weeks.

I turned off my screen, and Naomi did the same. She had joyful tears in her eyes. I'd never seen her like that. It was even more enchanting than her smile.

"You think it was sad?" I asked.

"No, you were right, it was beautiful." She wiped the tears away and sighed. "Sorry, I just did not expect you to pick something so…I don't know, something like that."

"Thanks, I guess. You know, I'm not all money and prestige."

"I do know. You are much more than that. I think you'll surprise even yourself with what you're capable of."

"What do you mean?"

Her face had its usual disarming smile, but she seemed guarded. "I just mean you have the brightest of futures," she said, "in ISA-7 or wherever."

The past came crashing back. "You passed the test, not me."

"But you will, next time." She put her hand on my cheek. "Let's not talk about ISA-7 this week. We're here to celebrate Easter and a wedding. It's going to be fun."

"It already is." I smiled. "But before we leave ISA-7 behind, I have to ask you about Charles."

Her mouth closed and tension crossed her composed face. "What about him?"

"You haven't told me anything beyond your one message. How did he die?"

"I don't know."

"I think you do."

"I don't know exactly what happened." She paused. "And you know that I can't talk about it. Everything about it is classified at the highest levels."

"Just tell me if you were with him before it happened."

She shook her head slowly. "Sort of…but not really." Tears were in her eyes again.

"Was Patrick with him?"

She nodded.

"When did it happen?"

"I can't say."

"A while before your message?"

She nodded again. "Why do you ask?"

"I saw him…after he died."

"*What!?*" Her face showed genuine shock. Our sync showed her pulse skyrocketing. "When?"

"Remember I told you I went to the Super Bowl?"

"Yes."

"He was my guest."

Her face hinted at her precept calculating something. She eventually breathed out, "That's impossible. You should have told me!"

"Who killed him?" I asked.

"We don't know," she said without hesitation. "What

did he say to you when you saw him?"

"A lot of things. He told me not to trust you."

"Oh God!" She lifted her hand from mine and put it over her mouth. Her eyebrows lowered in anger. "Someone must have been controlling his body. You know whatever he said was a lie, right?"

"I trust you." I left unsaid the "mostly" that I thought. "But it's hard not knowing, being on the outside. And why would anyone want to warn me?"

She took my hand again. "I know it's hard," she said. "That's why I didn't want to talk about it. And I don't know all the answers, far from it."

"What do you know?"

"I know losing Charles was a tragedy. I know the world's undercurrents are swirling, and I fear dangerous things will rise from these currents." She blinked slowly and then looked at me with a gentle, somber smile. "I know that, despite all those things, you and I were meant to be together in the days ahead. Can't that be enough for now?"

The way her face was set, I figured it had to be enough. I tucked away my questions about Charles. I focused instead on the present, on Naomi.

"Okay," I agreed, "but does this mean we have to spend a whole week in Italy falling madly for each other, instead of thinking about international crises and secret orders?"

She shrugged. "There's a decent chance."

"Good, I like falling for you."

"I might say the same, especially after that movie." She

leaned her head on my shoulder. Her honey curls fell down over my chest. "But we better sleep if we hope to enjoy the Easter service tomorrow. It's going to be special."

"I like that plan." I leaned my head over to rest on hers.

We were quiet then. She fell asleep within moments. It took me longer, but I slept all the same.

33

We landed in Rome at 7:15 am, Easter morning.

I'd always been amused by Easter, and not just because of the pastel bunnies. People like Naomi picked this random day every year to celebrate a guy rising from the dead. *Rising from the dead.* It had always made me laugh. Before Charles anyway. Sure, science could make us live to 150. We could transfer every organ except the brain, and that was around the corner. But nobody could rise from the dead. Dead was dead. Even though I'd seen Charles walking and talking after he died, it wasn't really him. Someone controlled him. No one could have pulled off that technology two thousand years ago.

But the airport was full of these people making their pilgrimage to hear the pope talk about a dead man. Looking at them, it wasn't that funny anymore. It was comedy with a sad ending, like a Shakespeare play.

"What's your favorite play by Shakespeare?" I asked Naomi. We had reached the airport's line for country entries. It would be a long wait.

"Shakespeare?" She raised her eyebrows. "You're full of surprises. Want me to say *Romeo and Juliet*?"

"No, I want you to say your favorite."

"*Macbeth*. It shows the tragedy of sin. How about you?"

"*Hamlet*." If she'd given me ten choices, I would not have picked Macbeth for her. "*To be, or not to be...in love*." I recited.

She smiled. "I think you added something."

"It's implicit," I said, stepping forward in the line. At least it was moving quickly. "Don't you get some special pass for lines like this?"

"I wish," she said. "Remember, though, I'm a normal citizen on this trip."

"Normal like me?"

"I doubt that. Can't you buy your way past all this?"

"There are a few things money still can't buy."

"You would know." She laughed as a security guard pointed us toward a booth for scanning our chips. Two people remained in front of us. "What else can't money buy?" she asked.

"Skipping the country-entry line, eternal life, and true love. I think that's about it."

It was my turn at the booth. I held my wrist up to the scanner. The guard was watching a screen in front of him. I told him where I was staying and for how long. He didn't seem to care. He glanced up at me, pressed a button, and then waved me on.

I moved forward and waited for Naomi. She held her slender wrist up to the scanner. The guard's eyes went wide as he watched the screen. A red light started blinking above his booth.

Two more guards approached, electric guns in hand. One of them said something to Naomi, and she walked off between them. She waved to me as if this was all normal.

But then our sync disconnected. I waited there at least ten minutes, pacing, before the sync blinked on. A moment later Naomi came back. She was breathing heavily and her face was flushed. The top button of her shirt, which was done before, was undone.

"What happened?" I asked.

"They searched me." She breathed deeply, as if to calm herself. "Everything is fine. Let's go."

"Did they strip search you?"

"It doesn't matter." Her voice dropped to a whisper. "It's ISA. We agreed not to talk about it. You said there would be a car waiting for us?"

"Yes," I said, following her lead as she walked toward the airport exit. "Our bags will be delivered to the driver. But why did the security guys pick you out?"

"I'm not sure." She did not meet my eyes. "You remember they warned us about airport searches during training, right?"

"I guess so."

"Well, this was nothing unusual, and they didn't learn anything. They just think I'm normal ISA personnel. I think that's all." She grabbed my hand and walked faster. "Come on, Rome waits!"

I almost had to run to keep up with her long strides as she rushed out of the airport. Glass doors opened onto a warm pre-dawn and a line of black cars. A man with a black suit and black hat was standing beside one with a big card saying Goldsmith.

"There's our ride," I said. "Shall we?"

"We shall!" Maybe she thought her enthusiasm would make me forget that two Italian guys had just made her undress for a strip search. I added it to the growing list of mysteries.

We got in the car and began cruising into Rome. Naomi rolled the windows down and leaned her head out slightly. Her hair blew behind her in the wind. Her face was beautiful in the early morning light.

I looked out my window and watched the city. The further we went towards the center, the more removed we were from the modern world. Everything was marble and tile and stone. I saw hardly any trace of steel as we crossed the Tiber River and approached our hotel.

We checked in and dropped off our bags, with just enough time in the lobby for me to soak up the five-star air and swallow a shot of espresso.

The crowds would already be gathering for the Easter ceremony. So we headed out, toward the Vatican.

34

The sun was still low on the horizon when we left the hotel and joined the masses streaming along Rome's streets. The sky was a brilliant orange-red, casting all the marble in a hue that hinted at blood. If my dreams were coming true, I figured we were sheep going to slaughter. Everyone seemed excited. Energy filled the air.

We squeezed through the entrance to the Vatican and the piazza. The vast area was already packed, so we found a place to stand by one of the columns furthest from the basilica. As we waited there, the colorful sky began fading into a normal blue. My dream had dark clouds, and none of those were to be seen. Or maybe my dream had started with a blue sky? Not that I was worried. "How much longer do we have to wait?" I asked Naomi.

"Maybe half an hour." She was gazing at the basilica on the far side of the piazza. "Isn't it beautiful?"

The impressive dome was shining in the morning sun. "Yeah, and it looks just like it did in my dreams."

She turned to me. "You're still thinking about that?"

"What else am I supposed to think about? I remember standing in pretty much this exact spot, but I've never been here before. This is surreal."

"It is a clear morning, Easter morning. If what you've seen comes true, I will still trust in the Lord." She swept her arm out towards the crowd. "So will many of these people, and maybe you will, too."

"What do you mean?" It sounded like she fully expected what I'd seen to happen. "You're the one who wanted to come for this," I added. "Shouldn't we have stayed away if disaster is coming?"

"This is where we're supposed to be, Elijah. Right now, enjoy it with me while we can. This place is spectacular. Did you know they started building St. Peter's Basilica over five hundred years ago? The saint himself is buried deep inside its tombs." There was a zealous excitement in her voice.

"I've heard that," I said. "Bart told me the Romans killed Peter on a cross, hung him upside down. If you're both right, I think it's pretty ironic that he ends up buried here."

"Ironic?" She looked offended.

"Yeah, the Romans kill the guy, then he gets some special burial in the capital of the empire. Then the church goes on killing opponents for centuries, the crusades and all that. Next thing you know, they'll move Mohammad's bones to these tombs to start the next cycle."

She sighed. "Can we just wait in quiet and try to savor this moment?" Without waiting for an answer, she crossed her arms and turned away from me.

I wished I hadn't opened my mouth. I'd really been doing a good job tolerating her faith, I thought. There were more important things, like love. We'd figure it out.

My legs started getting tired while we waited in silence. It was an awkward silence, especially with all the people around us talking. I tried to count the different languages to pass the time. I heard five I knew and seven I didn't. I wondered how many were Jewish like me.

Naomi still had her arms crossed when the Pope finally walked out. He looked like a little pearl from where we stood. The stone piazza and basilica formed the oyster shell around him. Two giant screens to his sides zoomed in on his face of pale wrinkles and bright, beady eyes.

He held up a cross and began to speak. At first I didn't understand a word of it. I'd forgotten this service would be in Latin. V caught up quickly, translating the words, but I'd missed the very beginning.

"What did he say at first?" I asked Naomi.

"He is beginning the Easter mass, saying the rites." She kept her eyes on the Pope. "He invokes tradition."

Welcome to the celebration of the resurrection, V translated. It was amusing to hear her Australian voice speaking the Pope's words. *Praise the Lord that we can celebrate this Holy Mass...*

He spoke on and on, calling everyone to put faith in

Jesus, calling for hope built on the rock which is God, calling for more religious stuff. I heard the words, but as each moment passed, I felt my dream slipping away. Maybe the tiniest part of me had actually thought it would happen, even if I could never want such a thing. An hour drifted by. The sky was still blue. The world still spun. My dream was nothing more than a dream. Nothing special.

And in closing, the Pope said, *I pray for the intercession of the Virgin Mary and the saints, that the Holy Spirit may protect your souls and guide your vision. Amen.* The little pearl of a man stopped speaking and lifted his cross.

The ground seemed to shake. Just a little shake. My legs were probably tired from standing so long.

But then another tremor. Not an earthquake. Was it just my imagination?

People around us started murmuring.

"Did you feel that?" I asked.

Naomi looked at me. This time her eyes were alert, alarmed, like someone who's had way too much coffee.

"It's coming," she said.

Suddenly the sky was growing dark behind larger-than-life clouds. Wind began to gust.

"I thought you said—"

The ground started shaking again. There was no missing it this time. It trembled like jelly under my feet.

People started running and screaming. I staggered back just as someone collided with me. Our legs tangled and I fell to the side, my shoulder banging into a column. I was on the ground when I heard the sound. My heart froze.

It was the groan, the same deep groan from deep in the earth. Then, *CRACK*.

Everything happened exactly as I'd seen it, like when you're watching a movie for the tenth time. Except now I was awake, and my spinning questions and doubts crashed onto something hard: reality.

A lightning bolt struck, sudden and severe. It hit the cross at the top of the piazza's obelisk. Its flash was emblazoned in my eyes.

The cross smoked and leaned and crashed down. The crack through the middle of the piazza began to widen. Then, like a rubber band pulled taut and snapping apart, the piazza split open. The huge chasm swallowed hundreds of people. Their screams echoed and then were gone in the blackness below.

I felt a tug at my arm. It was Naomi, standing over me. She helped me to my feet, her face afraid but determined. We turned to run out, but then the ground shook violently again, knocking us both to our knees.

We watched in shock as the splitting earth spread to the basilica. I knew what was coming, but I still doubted it until the cracks rippled over the dome. The building wavered, swaying as if fighting gravity. But it lost the fight. The dome imploded and then the whole mass collapsed. A cloud of dust and debris mushroomed toward us.

I wanted to believe the creature wasn't coming next.

I wanted to believe it was just a dream.

But I had to believe my eyes when the shape rose from the chasm. Huge oily claws grabbed the lip of the gaping cliff, then the creature leapt into the air and unfurled its wings. Where the obelisk had been, the black dragon-like creature now hovered. Its giant wings flapped smoothly, holding its position like a seagull on a steady ocean wind. Its body was slender and smooth, more snakelike than I remembered, with sinister shadows coiling and wisping around it. The dragon's face looked eerily thoughtful...and hateful.

The few people still scattered around the piazza didn't seem to notice the creature. Some were huddled over fallen bodies, but most were rushing out of the square without a look back, away from the destroyed basilica and the chasm.

One tall, lean figure in the piazza looked calm. He walked toward the dragon. It fixed its red eyes on the man as if seeing an old friend. The dragon suddenly spoke words I could not understand. They sounded like grunts, but the man paused and nodded as if he knew their meaning. This time I knew who the man was. He was Abaddon, Don Cristo, President of the UN, and he was turning to me.

I tried to stand, to run, but my body did not budge. It felt paralyzed.

"Elijah." It was Naomi's voice. She was beside me.

"Elijah," she repeated. "Remember what Bart said. Remember what my mother said."

I had never told her about her mother, but I hardly had time to think about that. I remembered: *you must go, you must protect her, do not let him touch you*. That was what her mother had said.

"We can't move," I said.

"I know. He's here."

"Naomi." Don was standing over us. He looked even more magnificent in person, and his smile was ecstatic. How could harm come from him? I sensed this was a man who could give me whatever I wanted.

"Nooo…" Naomi strained to say the word.

"My dear Naomi. This will go better for you if you stay silent." He placed his finger over her lips and gazed down into her eyes.

Her lips looked sealed tight. Their normal luster became a pale thin line across her terrified face.

"There now, isn't that better?" he asked. "I have known for so long that it would be you, Naomi. So brave, so beautiful, so innocent, so like *his* mother." He spoke the word "his" with spewing venom and disgust, but then his face was smooth again, like a man who has passed by an intolerable stench. "How does it feel to be *my* chosen? Would you feel *my* touch?"

"Abaddon," the word bubbled out of me. I was desperate to free Naomi from his gaze.

"Elijah!" he said, gleaming with pride. "It is good to see you again, much better than dreams, don't you think?" His voice was smooth and welcoming. He held out his hand to me. "Remember, call me Don."

I reached up to shake his hand.

"*NO!*" Naomi screamed through barely open lips.

Don turned to her, but he spoke to me. "This is a chosen woman, Elijah. But you already know that, don't you? Now I will touch one of you. Should it be you, or her?" he mused.

Naomi was silent, but her face contorted with rage and fear. Her lips looked glued together again.

Do not let him touch you, I remembered.

"Touch her," I said, with no clue what it would mean.

"Wise choice." Don held out his hand. He inched it forward, toward Naomi's petrified face. The only part of her that moved was her eyes. They flipped about wildly, as if watching a swarm of gnats buzzing before her face.

Then Don knelt down and pressed his hand against her stomach, and Naomi's eyes closed. Don's other hand went to her forehead, and then reached for her waist. With both hands around her, he lifted her effortlessly and pulled her close to him.

"See," he whispered to her, "that was not so bad."

Her eyes were still closed. She sagged against his body.

"What's happening?" I asked. I was not afraid, even though I had every reason to be. It was as if this man had power to terrify *and* to soothe. He was soothing me, and I could not stop him.

Don turned to me. He looked amused. "Haven't they been teaching you, Elijah? You're the only who *could* know. I will help you in time, if you survive. My friend is hungry." He glanced over his shoulder at the dragon. "And more friends are coming soon. You two better run along now."

He leaned Naomi's limp body against my shoulder. Her eyes were starting to blink open as he turned and walked away, toward the chasm and the dragon.

I noticed then that the piazza was empty. Where thousands had stood just minutes ago, now there was no one left. Just Don, Naomi, a dragon, and me.

I pinched myself. I rubbed my eyes. Nothing happened. I was still awake. My breath caught and my heart raced. All I knew was that this was real, and I had a feeling Naomi had known that all along.

35

"What happened?" Naomi murmured, with her eyes half shut and almost all her weight on me. "I can't remember anything after he was walking toward us."

"He touched you." I didn't know what else to say. Don was nowhere to be seen. I tried to bring up V, to check Naomi's vitals. Nothing showed. My precept worked, but was no longer connected. I felt like a medieval explorer without a compass or a map. "Can you walk?" I asked. "We have to get out of here."

"I can walk with your help."

I took a step to go, her arm draped heavy over my shoulders. Then I heard a horrific sound all around me, so loud it felt like it came from inside my head—the dragon's roar. The creature flapped its wings and eyed us as it rose in the air.

It suddenly flew straight at us.

I dove with Naomi to the side of the closest column. The dragon's head slammed into it and knocked the enormous stones over. It roared and took flight again.

I scooped Naomi up into my arms and ran. I ran as fast I could, my heart pounding. I saw no sign of the creature once we were outside the piazza. The broad street leading out of the Vatican, the Via della Concilizione, was in chaos. But it was oddly comforting. At least there were other people here. No one acted as if they'd just seen an enormous flying serpent. It was like a normal disaster scene, I guessed, having never actually seen one in person before.

The ground rolled under my feet again, though not as bad as before.

"Another earthquake!" shouted someone.

People were sprinting and scattering like ants under the shadow of a boot. I kept on running. The buildings around us wobbled. Several had already collapsed and lay in ruins. The sky was still darkened by clouds overhead, but the lightning had relented.

We were halfway between the Vatican and the Tiber River when I stopped to catch my breath. I could not carry Naomi much longer. I set her down and tried to pull up V. This time there was nothing at all. I pressed my wrist for a manual reload. I issued the reboot command. Nothing.

Suddenly I realized how slow and bland my mind felt. It was like a plain potato, robbed of the fixings.

I took a deep breath and picked up Naomi. She did not protest. She just looked up at me with a faint, pained grin. "Thank you," she whispered.

I carried her toward a nearby row of parked scooters. Two guys were yanking on their wires, trying to jump-start them. Good thing Rome still had scooters old enough to hot wire.

"Can you help us?" I asked a wiry, dark-haired man who looked like he knew what he was doing.

He lifted his eyebrows, shook his head, then kept working on the wires of a rusted, lime-green scooter.

I tried Italian, "*Potete aiutare?*"

He glanced up, with understanding on his face.

"*Gli darò oro.*" My words came out choppy without V's help, but nothing about my watch did. It was gleaming *oro*, gold. I held it out of his reach and pointed at the scooter.

"*Bene*," he said with a smile.

His weathered hands took up the wires again and seconds later the motor was running. I gave him the watch, and he turned to work on the next scooter in the line.

I helped Naomi onto the seat and sat in front of her. "Hold tight, okay?"

"Okay, get us out of here." Her voice was distant, but her grip around my waist was tight.

I'd never ridden one of these things, but I figured it was like riding a bike. It wasn't. The throttle was tight. The engine sputtered and jerked as I tried to accelerate. It took every ounce of my focus to navigate through the debris littering the streets. But I made it work, riding as fast as I could toward the Tiber River. I wanted out of Rome and following a river seemed like my best bet.

Once I reached the Tiber, traffic was jammed everywhere. I kept to the sidewalks, dodging people, café tables, and chunks of fallen buildings. The muddy water flowing beside us was raging and churning like a flash flood. A few lifeless bodies were riding along the foam waves.

"There…" Naomi pointed to a sign for a highway.

"E80?"

"Mm hmm, to Fiumicino." She sounded hurt, or sick, or maybe worse.

"What's wrong? What did you feel when he touched you?"

"Just go," she said, leaning her head against my back. "I need you."

I nodded and forged ahead, following the signs to the highway. Within minutes, and after a few near crashes into poles and people and cars, we were on the highway.

It was a parking lot. People had stopped their cars and gotten out. They were shouting and panicking. I carved through the crowd like I was a drone in an ISA-7 test. They were just obstacles in my path, and my goal was to reach the port city of Fiumicino. I hoped Naomi knew what she was talking about.

We eventually reached a huge pileup of cars blocking the road. I swung to the far right, by the road's barrier, and barely squeezed through. My knee scraped against the concrete, ripping a hole in my jeans and drawing blood. A small price.

The highway was clear from there. The wind whipped

at me, the sky boiling overhead, as I accelerated the little scooter.

While we zoomed along, I tried to make sense of what had just happened. My dreams had been real. The dragon and the man, they were real, too. Don had touched Naomi. It had done something to her, but what? It was just a touch. How had it so affected her? I still felt like I was going to wake up soon.

After a short while, Naomi squeezed my shoulder. "Here. This exit."

I turned off a ramp from the highway. It was the exit for the Fiumicino airport. The sea was not far in the distance.

"Left here," she said. "Stay on this road another mile."

I followed her directions even though they led us away from the airport. I trusted that she had a plan. Was it something from ISA-7?

We drove into the port city, where the scene was the same as in Rome, if on a smaller scale. People were in the streets, in disarray, amid piles of crumbled buildings.

After Naomi directed me through another five turns, she pointed me toward a narrow alley. The alley led to an inlet tucked tight between buildings on either side. A thin dock reached out into the water. Two men in military fatigues were standing there with automatic rifles. Floating behind them was a sleek, charcoal-colored yacht.

"What now?" I asked.

"Follow me." Naomi slid off the scooter. She almost fell as she tried to stand. I moved quickly to her side and held up her weight again.

She stepped forward unsteadily with her arm on my shoulders, leading us toward the two military guys. They were pointing their guns at us.

"*Pare*," demanded one of them.

"*Omega*," she answered, like it was an order.

They nodded and exchanged a quick glance. One of them rushed to the boat at the end of the dock.

"What is going on?" I asked Naomi.

"We can get away." She pointed to the boat, as if that explained everything.

"Get away from what? Where are we going?"

She turned to me with a soft, shaken look. Her eyes were darker than I remembered. Her eyelids dropped, and she leaned her forehead against mine and closed her eyes. "I'm tired, Elijah. Just stay with me."

"Of course," I said, "but what—"

"Naomi!"

A man was rushing down the dock toward us. He wore a plain brown robe and had a ring of dark hair around his bald head. He looked like a modern Friar Tuck.

I stepped between Naomi and the friar as he approached. He stopped short of us and smiled, holding his hands out innocently.

"It's okay," Naomi said, "he's on our side."

"What is *our* side?" I asked.

The man burst into laughter, as if I'd said the funniest thing in the world. "This must be Elijah, eh?"

Naomi nodded. "We made it."

"Elijah, we're the good guys," said the man. His accent marked him as Italian. "I am Apollos Donatelli." He bowed slightly.

"How did you know my name?" I asked.

"Naomi told me about you. Please, now, come quickly. Time is of the essence." He stepped past me and took Naomi's hand. The smile fled from his face, replaced by a look of fear.

"What happened?" he asked, as he slid her other arm over his shoulders.

Naomi shook her head, her lips pressed tight together. With her arms draped over Apollos and me, she stepped along the dock, toward the boat.

We walked up the ramp and into the vessel. It was almost as big as my dad's yacht.

I considered stopping before stepping on board, to

demand more information. But what was I going to do? Wait around in this port town without even V to help me? Wherever we were going, I figured it would at least get me away from this disaster zone. I kept my mouth shut and followed Naomi's lead. I was not going to leave her.

The two men with guns boarded after us and pushed a button by the door to draw the ramp closed. They looked to Apollos, ready to obey.

"*Patmos, come previsto,*" Apollos said.

They nodded and marched away with their guns slung over their backs.

Friar Apollos led Naomi and me down a tight corridor. We came to a sitting room with a couch, several chairs, and a wide window looking out the back of the boat. Apollos and I helped Naomi lay down on the couch. Her body sank into its white leather.

"Get her some water," Apollos said to me, pointing to a small bar in the corner.

As I did so, he knelt beside Naomi, put his hand over her forehead, and closed his eyes. He began whispering something in Latin. I noticed a ring on his thumb. He had to be in the order, like Bart and Chris.

The boat's engines roared to life and we started moving. Water was a good idea. My mouth was bone dry, probably from all the dust I'd inhaled. I filled a glass for Naomi and one for me.

Apollos stayed kneeling over Naomi. I put her water down beside him and sat in one of the plush chairs. I downed my water and waited in quiet. Naomi seemed to be sleeping.

"So," I eventually said, "we're going to Patmos, as planned?" Apollos looked up at me. "Why Patmos?" I asked. "What was planned?"

"You speak Italian?"

"A little." I spoke everything with V. Without her, I could get by with Italian, Spanish, French, and Hebrew.

Apollos moved to sit across from me, leaving Naomi asleep on the couch.

"We are going to pick up someone on the island of Patmos. The man we will meet there, a holy man, he will have questions for you. You will answer honestly, no?"

"Maybe." I looked to Naomi, wondering what she had dragged me into. Her chest rose and fell smoothly. Her clothes were covered in dirt and some blood, as were mine. "I don't even know what to say." I turned to Apollos. "Is Naomi going to be okay?"

He nodded. "I think so. She seems to be in some form of shock. There is no major wound. What happened to her?"

I felt a pang of guilt, mixed with relief that he thought it was just shock. "It's hard to explain. But I guess she's been weak ever since Don Cristo touched her. He must have done something." But why had my dreams told me that was supposed to happen?

"Hmmm." Apollos rubbed his chin. "Yes, I believe she will recover, but this may change things."

Strange answer, I thought. I'd just told him the UN President had touched Naomi, and he hardly seemed surprised. I asked, "Why don't you tell me what's going on?"

"Much of it is obvious," Apollos said. "A massive earthquake struck Rome, causing great destruction. Naomi led you to me, because she knew I could get you to safety. We ride to Patmos, a special place in these trying times. We will be there in no more than a day, thanks to my swift vessel and her strong crew." He gestured proudly to the boat around us. "After we meet with the wise man on Patmos, and you tell us what you see there, then we travel on to meet others in a safe place. You should rest now, sleep as Naomi does. You arrived in my country just this morning, no?"

"A few hours ago," I said, rubbing my eyes. "You know this was not just an earthquake. What I saw back there was no mere trembling of the ground. What do you think is going on?"

"Many earthquakes. Signs of the end times." Apollos shrugged as if that was all there was to say. "Look, I will show you."

He pressed his wrist and a screen blinked on. I pressed my wrist, hoping V's connection was fixed, but still there was nothing. "How did you—?"

"Watch now," he interrupted, holding one hand up to me, and the other hand pointing at the screen.

My breath stopped. It was Don Cristo.

"...why I left my meeting in Geneva," he was saying.

"Did you declare an emergency then?" asked a woman in a practiced, broadcast voice.

"Yes, of course." Underneath Don's face was the text: *Don Cristo, President of the United Nations (Live)*. I'd been right beside him two hours ago, and now he was on a live broadcast. He was wearing the same dark gray suit and red tie, without a trace of dust. "We've had seven major earthquakes in a single day," he explained. "The earth groans, and we're doing everything in our power to save people, to bring help to those suffering."

"Let's start with Rome, your home city." The interviewer's face appeared on the screen, in a small window in the corner. It was a pretty face framed by pretty blonde hair, but it looked plain and mortal beside Don's. "You went there first after you left Geneva?"

"I did, I went to Rome." There was passion in Don's polished voice. He sounded compelling and sincere. "The harm there is immense. My heart weeps with my city. We have lost many lives. We have lost many relics. Even the great St. Peter's Basilica has fallen."

The woman wore a look of deep adoration. "I am so sorry, Mr. President," she said. "Where else have you been today? Please, I know it is hard, but tell us, tell the people of the world what you have seen. What can we do?"

"I went to Tokyo, then Jakarta, then..."

"What is he talking about?" Naomi asked. She was leaning up on the couch, resting on her elbow.

Apollos lowered the volume. "Don Cristo is broadcasting a message for the world," he said. "Billions are watching this. The UN's satellites are the only stable source of connectivity right now. Earthquakes destroyed seven cities today."

Naomi nodded. "It is as we feared."

"*As we feared?*" I asked with shock. "You sound so sure. You knew this was coming?" I could not believe that. Don's voice sounded like the only logical one in the room.

"Everything is okay, Elijah," Naomi said.

"No, it is not." I rose to my feet. "Everything is *not* okay. Why isn't anyone talking about the freaking dragon that just flew out of the ground?"

"*What?*" Apollos jumped to his feet.

"A dragon?" Naomi asked at the same time, confused. "What are you talking about?"

"You were right beside me," I said. "You saw it!"

She shook her head. "I saw the storm, the earthquake, and Don Cristo approaching. Trust me, if I'd seen a dragon, I would remember that."

I fell back into the chair and closed my eyes. *What was wrong with me?*

37

Apollos and Naomi were staring at me in wonderment.

"You saw it?" Apollos asked. "The dragon, the ancient serpent. What did it look like?"

I shook my head. If Naomi hadn't seen it, maybe I hadn't either. Maybe it was just a fragment of a dream.

"Chris and Bart, they were right." Apollos put his hand on Naomi's shoulder. He looked stunned, like the victim of a prank. "They were right, weren't they? It's not just symbolic."

Naomi nodded and turned to me. "Was it like in your dreams? Is that how the dragon looked?" She sounded better, as if healing from whatever had weakened her.

I kept my face blank. "You were right there. There's no way you could have seen Don and missed the dragon. You promise, you swear to God, you didn't see it?"

She shook her head. "I remember everything before

Don reached us—clear as day. But I promise I did not see a dragon or anything like that."

The problem was, I believed her. Only, she couldn't be right and I also be sane. I needed fresh air.

I walked to the wall of glass in the back of the room and slid open the door in the center. I stepped out, put my hands on the metal rail, and gazed over the sea. The shore of Italy was in the distance. We were going fast, really fast. The wind blew my hair into my face, so that the hair licked up the confused tears beginning to run down my cheeks.

"You are not crazy." Naomi came to my side and put her hand on mine. "I believe you. We all do."

Great, a crazy order believing in my crazy visions. I kept my gaze out over the water. I could not bring myself to look at her.

"You are special, Elijah. I told you that. Your dreams are special. As soon as you told me them, I suspected it. Bart and Chris believe you are a prophet."

"*A prophet?*" I laughed despite myself. "That might be more ridiculous than the dragon. I don't even believe in God." I turned to Naomi. Her serious face made me stop.

"I don't believe that," she said. "Especially not after what you saw today."

"It can all be explained."

"Really?"

"Yeah." My mind spun through the possibilities. "You don't remember Don touching you, right?"

"Right."

"Well maybe he touched me, too, and maybe I don't

remember it. He could have implanted a nanochip in each of us, somehow hacking into our precepts and our minds. It would be a way to track us and any data exchanged with us. It is no secret he wants to empower the ISA and have it under his complete control. He does not trust the U.S. branch. If he knew we'd been selected as fellows for ISA-7, we would be perfect for his monitoring." My words blasted into the salty air, and the more I said, the more I believed it. "Don could tap into everything about the ISA that is walled off from the UN. Imagine the power."

"That doesn't explain everything," Naomi countered. "Why would he come to us at the Vatican? Why during an earthquake? And what about your dreams?"

"Maybe the nanochip implanted in me includes the memory of the dreams. Maybe I never even had those dreams." Or maybe I had a tumor causing my visions, just like my mother. Naomi didn't need to hear that.

She was shaking her head. "You told me about your dreams. I remember."

A decent point. "Maybe your chip had that memory, too." This was starting to seem unlikely.

"You think, if Don really wanted to monitor us, he would put memories of a dragon in your dreams? How would that help?"

She had a point, again. But something about her questions gave me doubt. Had it somehow been Don who controlled Charles and told me not to trust her?

I calmed my voice and studied Naomi as I spoke. "So maybe those dreams were real, and maybe I'm just a little insane. That earthquake set Rome spinning, so maybe I saw things that weren't real. But Don said himself, in that interview, that he went to Rome. It would be the perfect ruse, the perfect opportunity, for him to insert a tracker in you. Why else would he pick you? Now he can monitor ISA-7."

"Don definitely did something to me." Naomi hesitated, glancing down at her body, her fingers pressed against her waist. "It could have been a nanochip. I'm not sure." She looked up, fear in her eyes. "The order believes the dragon and Don are somehow the devil incarnate, unbound and released to reign on earth for a little while. Based on your dreams and other signs, Bart thought we needed to be in the piazza together."

"Why us?"

"He thinks you're chosen to see, and I'm chosen by Don for something. Bart says you have to protect me. He said my mother told him the same thing before she died, about a Jewish boy from the Roeh line."

"So that's why you brought me into all this?"

"It may have started that way." She paused. "You know it's more than that now."

I met her eyes evenly. Her words seemed as true as any, despite all the pieces I didn't understand. Could she be the one thing I'd hold onto in the chaos? "But if what you said about the order and Bart is true, why would they leave us to face the devil on our own?"

"We're never alone, Elijah. Maybe you doubt it, but we have God on our side. The Alpha and Omega."

"I didn't see any god back there in Rome. All I saw was a dragon, the President of the UN, and a destroyed city."

"You're not looking in the right places," she said. "I have faith God will open your eyes. Your sight is distracted by this world, but it is powerful. I didn't see what you did."

"Maybe, I don't know." I shook my head. It was all too confusing; I couldn't lie to my own memory.

Naomi yawned. "I'm exhausted. Can we rest now, and talk more later?"

My body shouted agreement. We'd gone straight from a red-eye flight to a disaster scene. I could hardly think straight, but part of me was scared to sleep, scared to dream. Plus, as crazy as these theories sounded, I wanted to learn more.

As I hesitated, Naomi pushed windblown hair out of my eyes. "Please, let's rest now. I don't want to be alone."

"Okay, I'll stay with you." I tried to sound confident, while doubts kept flooding my mind.

I led her back inside the yacht, to a small cabin with a bed filling almost the whole room. We each collapsed onto it, fully clothed. She curled her knees up and I laid behind her, pressed close. Her lean limbs and back felt perfect against me. Her breathing began to steady and slow.

It was not long before I fell asleep.

The dragon met me there. It was perched on a mountain, far above me. Its smooth black skin seemed to grow out of the stones under its giant claws. The claws gripped like a vice, cracking the rocks. I felt that if it flew off, it would carry the whole mountain with it. The red eyes were fixed on me, and I stared back.

Then the dragon unfurled its wings. They were like a bat's wings, large enough to swallow the world. It twisted its long neck over its back. In that moment, while it looked away, I noticed an ocean below me, at the foot of the mountain. Its calm waters were blood red. The dark mountain, the red water, and the grey sky were like a deep, bruised wound on the earth.

When the dragon's head turned back to me, something was in its mouth.

I had to see what it was. I stepped forward. I had no choice. I started climbing the mountain. My hands and knees were scraped and bleeding, but I kept moving upward. The dragon waited for me. I knew now it was a *he*, and he would wait until I came. He *wanted* me to see.

As I reached the top, the dragon bared his man-sized razor teeth, almost like a smile. Like he was happy. No, he was delighted—delighted about whatever was in his mouth. He was proud of it. I knew it, and he knew that I knew it. His red eyes blinked slowly, and then his jaws parted.

There, in his mouth, was a baby.

The dragon's serpent tongue was curled around it, wrapped like a swaddling cloth. The tongue began to unwind, setting the baby down between the dragon's claws. The baby was naked and started to cry.

The dragon coiled its head back, snarled, and then struck at me like a snake.

I woke up shaking.

38

Naomi was shaking me. I rose on the bed. I was covered in sweat again, and I kept shaking even when Naomi moved her hand away.

"What did you see?" she asked.

It took me a moment to remember where I was. On a bed on a boat, racing through the Mediterranean Sea.

"I saw the dragon again." I rubbed my eyes, trying to wake up. "Do you have any water?"

"What else did you see?"

"Just the dragon." I met Naomi's stare. Why did she always have to look so eager? Still, her skin looked like it glowed in the morning light through the porthole. "What time is it?"

"7 am," she answered. "We are almost to Patmos. Come, Apollos will want to hear about your dream."

"I'm sure he will." I followed her out and down a hall

to the sitting room where we'd been the day before.

Apollos was there, talking to a well-dressed man. Trays of breakfast were laid on the table in the middle of the sitting area. I was starving, and still thirsty.

"Good morning, Elijah, Naomi." Apollos gestured to the food. "I hope you had a good rest. Please, sit and eat. We have less than an hour before we reach the island."

He did not have to tell me twice. I sat and began filling my empty stomach. Naomi sat beside me and did the same.

"You two went to sleep before we could finish our discussion yesterday, and before I could offer showers, clean clothes, and an introduction to my friend." He nodded to the man beside him. "This is Prince Gregory, the Duke of Wales."

I looked up, with my mouth stuffed full of a hard-boiled egg. It was him, the heir to the British royal throne.

"I," Naomi began with awe, "I knew you were in the order, but I didn't expect...I didn't." She started to stand. I stayed in my seat, trying to chew faster.

"Please, please, there is no need." He stepped forward and helped her to her feet. His blue, tailored suit had gold buttons and a purple silk pocket square to match his purple tie. The way he smiled at Naomi made me want to vomit. "We are on the same team here, on equal footing." He bowed and kissed her hand.

"What are you doing here?" I asked. They all turned to me with surprised looks. I must have sounded angry.

"Apollos and I are the European members of the order." He spoke as if his words were all the answer I needed. I glanced down at his hands. He had the same translucent thumb ring. "I have heard about you, Elijah."

"Really?" I rose slowly to my feet. It was getting hard to separate dream from reality. I wasn't sure whether it was weirder for the British prince or the UN President to know about me.

"Of course," he said. "I have heard much from Chris and from Bart. We are thankful to have found you. Your vision will be needed in the days ahead."

"Bart told you about the order, yes?" Apollos asked me.

"He mentioned the order of John. He did not say anything about the bloody Prince of England."

"Elijah!" Naomi said.

Gregory put his hand on her shoulder. "It's okay." He smiled at her again, an annoyingly charming smile to go with his annoyingly charming accent. "I know this must be hard to understand," he said to me. "We operate in teams of two, one public member and one private, a team for each continent. I trust my presence on this boat proves this is serious."

I nodded, at a loss for words.

"Then, it is an honor to meet you, Elijah." He held out his royal hand. I stared at it. "Your purpose is beyond even the order's comprehension."

I shook his hand, wondering what that was supposed to mean. As our hands separated, I suddenly felt uneasy, as if sick to my stomach. I could have sworn I saw Gregory's face *shift* for an instant, almost like a mirage. I blinked slowly. When my eyes opened, everything looked normal.

Maybe I needed a doctor.

"Very well," said Apollos. "We are almost to Patmos now. We will meet with John. He insists that we visit the cave before we leave for Jerusalem. He wants to know if Elijah sees anything unusual there. After that, we must begin to activate our plan."

"The plan," Naomi explained, "is to go into hiding for a while. We believe great destruction is coming."

"Like more earthquakes?" I asked. "Why?"

Naomi nodded. "Remember what Bart said?"

"Some of it." *Earthquakes, storms, meteors, you name it—*those were Bart's words. "I listened to him, but that man obviously has a few loose screws." I pointed to my temple to emphasize the point.

"Bart is one of our leading interpreters," Apollos said. "I admit he has some idiosyncrasies, but hasn't he been right so far?"

"Earthquakes in 2066," I shrugged, "that's an easy guess, if it's even a guess. Seismologists predicted more earthquakes would come, as the earth warms and the plates shift."

"I like this kid," Gregory said. "He's got a mind of his own. I've been saying all along we should be careful how much we listen to Bart. And better to fight than to hide."

"Gregory, please." Apollos sighed. "Let's not cover this again, not now. What Elijah saw proves Bart was right about the power, the position, and the dragon. Don is Abaddon, the destroyer and the prince of this world."

"You're putting a lot of faith in Eli." Gregory glanced

at me and spoke as if I was now a child to be ignored. This prince was all over the place. "He may be smart, but Naomi didn't see what he says he saw. What if he's wrong?"

"Bart trusted Elijah," Apollos asserted. "This is real."

Gregory's eyebrows raised in skepticism. "Elijah said it himself. No matter who Bart was in the past, he has been losing his mind lately."

"Enough!" Apollos's fists were shaking. "We'll not speak such words of each other."

Gregory regarded him coolly, looking almost amused.

"I saw the dragon." My quiet words filled the tense room. "Trust me, I wish I hadn't, but I did." I met Gregory's stare. There was something soothing about him, kind of like Don. "Still, even if I saw it, that doesn't make it real. We should believe in things that can be proven with evidence."

"Your dreams *are* real," Naomi said, "and so is what happened in Rome...so is whatever awaits in Patmos."

"Like the dragon, coming again?" I scoffed. "If so, maybe I'll sit out this time. I might be able to find a way to an airport to get us back to the U.S."

"Indeed he might," Gregory encouraged. "We should admit we have not been entirely honest with him."

"I *have* been honest," Naomi said. "Elijah, please, don't back away now."

I turned from Gregory to her. The same sick feeling covered me like a sheen of oil on water. My mind was racing, losing control. "Have you been planning this from the start?" I asked Naomi. "Just playing me, leading me along, so that your order can make me part of this scheme? And what about ISA-7? You know, my precept never found any trace of you having a friend from New Zealand named Jade. Was the whole wedding a lie?"

She looked like I'd stabbed her in the gut. I regretted the words, but I wanted the answer.

"No, it's not like that." She waved her delicate hands defensively. "I promise."

"Then what is it like?"

"It's like your dreams," Apollos interrupted. "There are layers of truth, and layers of meaning. Look, everyone, these are trying times, and we have a long road ahead. We all agree"—he shot a defiant glance at Gregory—"that the devil is returning and probably through Don. But there is much we do not understand. Elijah, John knows more than all of us about these prophecies. Once we get to Patmos, he will tell us more. Until then, how about a shower and a change of clothes?"

"I brought an extra suit," Gregory volunteered. "We're about the same size."

"Fine." I stood. "Where's the shower?"

Apollos led me there, away from Naomi. Once I was alone, I turned the water on cold and got in. Whatever it took to cool me down. I stood there, soaked and shivering and confused. The white marble floor of the shower turned into a brown puddle as the dust and blood washed away.

I stepped out and put on one of Gregory's suits. The fabric was a flawless khaki linen, the kind I used to wear when my family went to our house in the tropics. The prince had good taste, and we were the same size except the suit was a little tight in the shoulders.

I left the bathroom and headed out to the yacht's back deck, wishing I felt like a new man, or even a man at all. Instead I felt like a naïve boy, caught up in something too big to understand.

This time it didn't help that Naomi was there on the deck, waiting for me.

39

"I'm sorry," Naomi said.

She was radiant, in a yellow dress. Her hair looked darker. It was still wet from her shower, blowing lightly in the ocean breeze. The ship seemed to have slowed down.

"Thanks." I joined her by the railing, resolved to get some answers. "I need to know, has this all been a game from the start?"

She pushed back a lock of my curls, just as she had before. "I told you, the start doesn't matter anymore."

"It matters if it was a lie."

"What's a lie?" she asked. "People say there's black and white with gray in between. But that's wrong. There's only black and white. The trouble is, we don't always know which one is which."

"Was it a lie?" I pressed her. "Why did you invite me to come with you to the Cathedral?"

"It was black and white. I don't even know all the reasons."

"Then give me just one."

"Okay." She paused. "My precept ran the report on you, just as I'm sure yours did on me. It's amazing how much we share. I mean, the same birthday? What are the odds?"

"Not high," I said. "How about another reason?"

"Your dream, obviously."

"I still don't know how you dragged that out of me."

"I asked God to reveal what you were hiding," she said, "and whatever you ask in prayer, you will receive, if you have faith."

"Sounds nice, but I doubt that's true." It wasn't very assuring, anyway. "What about the wedding?"

She looked down. "There was supposed to be a wedding."

"What do you mean *supposed to be*?"

"You know now what I believed, that the wedding would never happen." She turned back and held me in a steady gaze. "Does any of that matter now? Stay with me, protect me, like you did in Rome."

I looked away, over the blue waves stretching to the horizon. I felt like screaming inside, but my voice came out cold and flat: "I won't protect someone who lies to me like you did."

"I said I'm sorry, and you're right." She breathed in deeply. "I was wrong to lead you on. I was wrong to bend the truth. But I hope you see now why I did it. It wasn't just for me, or for the order. It was for *you*." Her voice broke in the salty air. "And it was for us."

I kept my eyes on the water. I was not going to let her break me down. Not this time. "What makes you think there's an *us?*"

"I don't *think* it, I know it…and so do you. You can't deny there's something between us. I've tried denying it. I've told myself there's no way I can have these feelings for a guy who doesn't believe in my God. But no matter how many times I've said it, I've known it's wrong." Passion crested in her voice like the ocean waves below. "Somewhere along the way—between ice cream, the reflecting pool, the sync, and you saving me in Rome—I fell for you."

And I fell for you, I thought, but held back. My knuckles were white as I squeezed the railing, trying to stay behind my crumbling walls. "Fell for me," I said, "or for somebody you think is a prophet?"

"For you," she answered firmly. "You're no prophet yet, not when you doubt your creator, the very one who gave you the visions. But I believe in you, Elijah."

I gave in and turned to her, meeting her hurt and vulnerable gaze. Lines of dried tears were on her cheeks. She seemed as real and honest as I'd ever seen her. I sensed in my bones she was right: there was an *us*.

She pressed a finger onto my chest, as if there was some truth hidden inside me. "We'll find out soon enough," she continued. "I don't know what's coming. I'm scared about whatever Don did to me. I want you to be with me through this."

"Okay," I said, "but no more secrets, no more lies."

She nodded. "From now on, I'll tell you everything."

"Thank you. I'll do the same." I put my hand on the side of her porcelain neck. "And I forgive you."

She smiled and leaned her head on my shoulder. I held her tight. Our breaths were heavy, excited, relieved, united. It seemed like a moment that could go on forever, but then the sound of the engines stopped.

"Time to go," Apollos called through a window in the yacht's rear cabin. "Head to the front. We're landing."

Naomi stepped back and squeezed my hands. "Let's go."

I nodded and we walked together to the front deck, where Apollos, Gregory, and five armed guards were waiting. The late morning sun blazed over the sea. There was no trace of a cloud in the sky. The vessel was in a cove before a small beach and a rocky hillside.

"The sun appeareth!" Gregory looked Naomi up and down. I felt a strong urge to give his pretty face a black eye. "Simply magnificent. And the dress is quite fitting for this day."

"A bright day indeed," Apollos said. "Where is John?"

"We saw him, sir." One of the guards pointed his rifle up the hillside beyond the beach. "An old man was making his way down that path. He should arrive soon. Shall we cast off?"

"Yes, *andiamo*."

Two guards moved to the port side of the boat, where

a black raft was bobbing in the water. One of the guards hurried down a ladder by the boat's side, while the other began guiding our group. Naomi went first.

Gregory put his arm around my shoulder and spoke as if we were chaps. "You don't look so bad, yourself." We were the last two in line for the raft. "Sharp suit, I must say. You ready for this?" He posed the question with an action-movie tone.

"No." I shrugged his arm away. "But I'll manage. The suit's not bad. For a prince, I expected someone taller."

He met my eyes evenly, for the first time without a smile on his face, and looking sincere. It gave me the chills. "Expectations are a weak thing," he said. "In this game, you must come prepared."

A guard tugged at me. I climbed down the ladder and into the raft. Gregory followed a moment later, and we pushed off. One of the guards fired up the engines and we accelerated. We reached the shore in seconds, coasting straight onto the thin beach.

An old man was waiting there, alone. "Welcome!" he announced as we stepped out of the raft. The man had a full head of white hair, with a long white beard. He was like a model prophet from a children's Torah.

"You are a welcome sight." Apollos embraced him like a brother. "I feared you might not make it to this day."

The old man laughed at that, leaning heavily on a staff of gnarled wood. "God's righteous right hand holds my right hand." As the man raised his right hand off the staff and into the air, his body shook as if he would fall. "He says to us, fear not, I am the one who helps you." I breathed easier when he put his hand back on the staff.

But then my breath froze when his gaze passed over me. He had the blank, white eyes of a blind man. Yet he smiled at me, an unnerving, knowing smile. He turned then to Naomi.

"Dear child, I remember you well. I even remember your face," he said, like a grandfather. "As true and beautiful a face as I've ever seen. Now surely you stand as a young woman, a woman clothed with the sun." Was that a lucky guess about her dress? She was wearing yellow. "Please, come to me." He reached out to her.

She stepped forward and took his frail, withered hand into hers. "I remember, too," she said, raising his hand to her face. "You told me that you would be waiting for me here, but that you would never again see me. I am sorry for your loss."

"Loss?" The old man smiled as he gently ran his fingers over Naomi's face. "My eyes were tired. They had seen enough of this world. If God saw fit to let them blink out, who am I to consider that a loss? It is gain, just as you may gain even from an evil touch."

Naomi's eyes hinted at surprise. She opened her mouth to speak, but Gregory spoke first. "And such evil there is in the world today, Father John."

The old man's blind stare snapped to Gregory. His face suddenly looked sad. "You speak more truth than you know, Prince Gregory. In these days, even a close friend in whom we trust, who ate our bread, could lift his heel against us."

Gregory's smooth face showed no emotion, but he stood rigid as if in a battle line, as if ready to defend against the helpless old man. "We must be ready for anything," Gregory said.

"This is true," responded the old man. "Anything from above, around, *and* inside, yes?"

Gregory nodded in silence.

"But are we ready for *you?*" The old man turned to me.

"Um, hello." I had no idea what to say. "My name is Elijah Goldsmith." I held out my hand awkwardly. I let it fall to my side when I realized he couldn't see it.

"It is a pleasure to meet you, Elijah." The old man smiled and winked a blind eye at me. "My name is John." He stamped his staff into the ground. "Let's go, everyone. Holy ground awaits. Maybe there we'll see a hint of what's to come."

40

John led us up the rocky hillside. We stayed to a thin path between thirsty-looking shrubs. He climbed with surprising speed. A brisk enough walk to make my breathing heavy. Naomi chatted away with the others as if unaffected by the pace.

They spoke of the other members of the order. It sounded like they were planning to converge soon, somewhere near Jerusalem. Naomi talked about Bart and Chris, and she told me the names of the seven other leaders, from all regions of the world: Ronaldo, Vicente, Zhang Tao, Jacques, Mehmet, Emeka, and Neo. With John, Apollos, and Gregory, that made twelve total. Of course a secret order would have twelve leaders.

It was not long before the midday sun began to bake my pale face. My sunscreen was in a bag in a hotel in Rome, probably under a pile of rubble. Sweat poured out only to be whisked away by the ocean breeze through Gregory's fine linen suit. This was more adventure than I'd bargained for.

We were halfway up the hillside when the old man stopped. The rest of us halted behind him.

"Here we are," he said. He went prostrate and kissed the ground before entering a small white door. Apollos and Naomi and Gregory did the same. I walked through last, pausing for just a slight bow. I figured the ground had enough kisses.

Inside was a cave decorated with wood and gold carvings perfect for tourist pictures. The five of us were a tight fit in the little space, and the stone walls gave it the feel of a dungeon. The others had looks of awe on their faces.

"This is it?" I asked.

"This is a holy place," answered Apollos.

"I guess so. I see lots of crosses," I said.

Naomi took my hand. "The crosses mean something." Her eyes begged me to indulge in whatever was going on.

"Even if it is holy," I said, "that doesn't explain why we'd rush away from Rome just to end up here."

"What do you think happened in Rome?" John asked.

"An earthquake," I hesitated, "and something bigger."

"Much bigger," John said. "Bart has told me what you discussed with him. Did your dreams not prove true?"

"It's getting harder to separate dreams from reality." I looked to Naomi. How could she not have seen the dragon? "No one else saw anything unusual in Rome."

The old man nodded like he knew I was hiding something. He picked up a book from a wooden shelf by a wall of the cave. "Two thousand years ago, my namesake John saw unusual things, things no one else saw." He put his finger on a page of the book. I noticed even he was wearing one of those rings on his thumb. "The apostle saw a serpent unbound, a woman clothed with the sun, and a great white throne. Many think his visions are allegory, or crazy. Is that what you think?"

"Yeah, they sound crazy. Symbolic at best."

"Like your visions?"

"They are more than symbolic," I admitted.

"Because they proved to be true?"

"I don't know." I was running out of explanations.

"Care to guess why you're here?"

"Your order wants to know what I see...maybe because you think I'll tell you what's coming next."

"That's right," he said. "We have faith about the future, but that does not mean we know all the steps and their reasons. Here's what I believe: you're a seer, Elijah. You see what others cannot. In the days ahead, you must learn to act upon what you see." His words dripped out with the patience of pouring honey. "Seeing the truth is only a curse if you deny it or stand still and watch."

"Wise words," said an unknown woman's sultry voice. "And fine last words, though they'll do no good." She stood in the doorway, hands on her bare hips. Sleek black scales, like those of the dragon in Rome, covered her skin but revealed every curve of her perfect body. I could not move my eyes off her.

"What do *you* say, my little prince?" A forked tongue flicked out of her mouth, towards Gregory.

"The words will do no good," the prince mumbled in response. He stepped close to her. I found myself yearning to feel her touch, jealous as she ran her finger along Gregory's cheek.

"Aren't you going to introduce me?" she asked.

"This is Jezebel," he said to us. I broke my gaze away and was stunned to see Naomi and Apollos eyeing her with innocent smiles, as if she were a normal woman passing by.

Only John's useless eyes looked at her differently. He was wary, pressed against the back wall of the cave. His words came out firmer than iron: "I prayed it would not be you, Gregory. What was your price?"

"Me," Jezebel answered, smiling. Her teeth were like fangs, but with her sensuous lips, they threatened pleasure instead of pain. "It's not too late for the rest of you to switch sides." She stepped forward and beckoned to me.

I held out my hand. I wanted nothing more than to feel her touch. Her voice drowned out my other senses.

"Stop him." It was John's voice.

I heard the words as if in the distance. Jezebel's body filled my mind, my very existence. It beckoned me.

But suddenly Naomi was tugging me away. She looked plain, human, compared to Jezebel.

"Elijah, Elijah," Naomi was saying, "What's going on? What do you see? Something more than a tourist woman?"

Jezebel ran a finger between her breasts. "Come, Elijah,

I have something for you."

I stepped towards her, but Naomi gripped my arm firmly, holding me back.

"What do you see?" John asked. "Elijah, what does she look like?"

"Pleasure," I answered.

"Describe her," John demanded.

"Describe me," Jezebel invited.

I hardly recognized my voice as I spoke. I could not restrain the passion, even lust. "Her face and body are so dark, so perfectly chiseled."

"What?" Naomi's mouth gaped open.

"Tell us more," John said.

"She has bare onyx skin." Words began to roll out of my lips as if Jezebel were a muse summoning them. "Bare except for the smooth scales, hiding but revealing her hips, her waist, her breasts. Her mouth is danger and delight, a forked tongue and lips like a forbidden fruit. The little horns are—"

"Demon!" Apollos shouted. "How can this be? Away!" He was holding up a gold cross toward the woman.

"Shiny cross," she said. "At least you can look at that while you all die. Last chance, who wants to join Gregory and me? Who wants to live? Who wants *me*?"

"No," whispered Naomi in my ear, still holding my arm tight. "*Elijah!*"

The way she said my name broke something, like a dark glass sphere around me cracking and light shining through. I stepped back from Jezebel, whose eyes were glowing coals. "What are you?" I asked. "How—"

"In the name of Jesus Christ," John interrupted, his ancient voice as solid as the cave walls. "You shall have none of us. You know our Lord will prevail."

Jezebel bellowed out a deep, harsh laugh. Carnal waves rippled through her curved figure.

A loud crack from outside silenced the room.

"The true lord is coming now." Her smile was gone. All of her allure turned to terror. Fear and shame gripped me. "You will all die." She pointed at me. "This battle has just begun."

Then the ground started shaking.

41

"Out, now!" Apollos charged toward the door leading out of the cave, with his cross held out toward Jezebel.

I moved to follow but stumbled when the ground lurched. Jezebel struck Apollos like a snake. She grabbed his outstretched arm and snapped it over her knee. The cross fell to the ground and Apollos screamed in pain.

Jezebel turned to Gregory and slid her forked tongue into his mouth. His face was in ecstasy, his eyes blazed. Jezebel pulled back and fled out of the cave.

Gregory stood blocking the door. Apollos was on his knees, groaning over his broken arm.

The ground shook again, harder.

"We have to go," John said. Stones began to tumble from the rock walls and ceiling above.

Naomi stepped forward. A small, gleaming gun was in her hand. Where had that come from?

"Let us out," she demanded to Gregory.

"My ray of sunshine," he said, his eyes still burning fires. "I'm afraid I cannot do that."

"Three." She pointed the gun at his head. He blinked but stood his ground.

"Two."

There was a roar outside. I knew the sound. The dragon.

"One."

She lowered the gun and...*crack!*

The sound exploded in the room and Gregory fell, screaming and grabbing his leg.

Naomi kept her gun pointed at him while she motioned for the rest of us to leave. John and Apollos hurried out, and Naomi and I followed.

A vast chasm split the island in two. The dragon was hovering in the air over the chasm, wrapped in shadows. Its red eyes glared at us just as in Rome.

"You all see that?" I asked, pointing at the monster while it flapped its gigantic, sinuous wings.

"Another earthquake," said Naomi. "The ground is ripped open. We have to get back to the boat." She sounded every bit like an ISA-7 agent, and not at all like someone who saw a dragon in the sky.

"What do you see?" John asked. His blind eyes seemed to be studying me.

"The dragon, or serpent, or whatever you call it." I pointed at the creature. "It's right there."

"So he *is* unbound." John's solemn voice matched his

white-haired visage. "Naomi is right, we have to get to the boat. We cannot fight him. He will only destroy and torment until he is conquered."

"This way," Apollos grunted, clutching his broken and bleeding arm. He started down the path we had followed up to the cave. John went second, Naomi was third, and I was last. We moved at a quick walk, as fast as John's aged legs could go.

Halfway down we had to step over the body of one of the guards. Blood puddled around him, and a boulder was on the ground by his side. There were no cliffs over us. It was as if the huge rock had been thrown at the man.

We kept going and turned a corner so that the vessel came into view in the cove. Jezebel was standing on the sandy shore, between the raft and us. Her hand was on her hip, waiting and daring us to approach.

"I'll fight her," Naomi said. "Apollos, you and John get to the raft."

"I'll fight, too," I volunteered.

"No." Naomi sounded adamant. "She has power over you, because you can see her true form. All I see is a bland, dark-haired woman."

"I'm not leaving you. I am your vision. Do you have another gun?"

Naomi shook her head, but Apollos pulled one out of his robe. It was long and thin, with a charge pack by the trigger and Chinese characters. An automatic laser rifle. China was rumored to have equipped its drones with these.

"Here." Apollos held it out to me. "My right arm is

broken. Take it."

I took the gun. Its weight in my hands made me feel stronger—probably false security.

"You cannot kill her," John explained, "but you can resist her. Any resistance against her will weaken her." He pressed his finger to my forehead and made the sign of a cross. "To avoid her allure, close your eyes if you must. We will slip behind her while you fight, then you must join us."

Our group split then, with Naomi and me walking straight towards Jezebel. She moved forward to meet us.

"I like you, Elijah," Jezebel taunted. "That's why I'm going to give you another chance. Let me take your girlfriend and these two worthless priests, and I'll let you ride my father and, if you're lucky, me."

Naomi shot her gun and hit Jezebel between the eyes. The demon woman staggered back, but the hole from the wound sealed over in black and she stood straight again.

"Not nice, sun girl," growled Jezebel. This time she sounded nothing like a temptress. "You know we are rivals. Won't you let me play with your pet boy?"

"Your words will not affect me." Naomi fired her gun again. "I do not need to see your true form to know you for what you are."

I raised the gun to my shoulder, looked down the barrel, aimed at Jezebel's chest, and pulled the trigger. With only a slight quiver, a red line suddenly beamed out. Its path was true. It hit the demon right where her heart would be, if she had one.

"*No!*" she screamed, glaring at me. She staggered

forward with a grimace on her face. The laser fired through her and out her back, but still she advanced. The beam was like a rope, tugging her closer.

Crack, crack, crack.

Naomi unloaded on her. The three shots made Jezebel fall. As she did, the laser beam split her open like a zipper undone through her shoulder.

I let go of the trigger, and the red beam disappeared. Jezebel was a sizzling pile of broken blackness on the ground.

Naomi took four swift steps to stand over the pile. Her taut, outstretched arm fired the rest of the bullets down into the smoldering remnants.

The smoke from the tip of Naomi's gun swirled and mixed with the fumes from Jezebel's twitching, destroyed body. Part of me cringed at the loss of that physical beauty, but most of me wanted to run somewhere, anywhere away from here, as fast as I could possibly run.

A rush of wind engulfed us and stopped me before I could make a move. The dragon soared overhead and landed just above us, on the bottom of the hillside. Its landing sent a cascade of huge stones rolling down at the beach and us.

As we scrambled away, Apollos was charging back towards us. He threw Naomi to the side just as the stones crashed down. An instant later a boulder rolled over him, exactly where Naomi had been standing. His brown robe was motionless. Blood pooled out from under his crushed body.

Naomi cried out at his side. I fell to my knees in shock.

"Come, now!" John shouted. He was standing in shallow water by the raft. Two guards were there now, with guns raised to the sky, nowhere near the dragon.

Now I was convinced. They could not see the creature, and I most certainly could. No figment of my imagination could send boulders crashing like that, killing Apollos.

Naomi raced for John, and I followed after her. A glance back over my shoulder showed the dragon taking flight again.

It swooped low, inches from our heads, and landed in the water beside the raft, the guards, and John.

Its giant mouth sneered at me.

"*No!*" I shouted.

"*What?*" Naomi's voice sounded desperate, terrified.

"The dragon…" I said, pointing at the creature. Its movements were strange, gradual then twitching, like a spirit possessed or a leaf whipped around in the wind. I almost expected it not to be able to touch the men, but when it flung its wings out, the guards were flicked away like marbles. Their bodies splashed far into deeper water.

John turned his head to where the men had been, but he had no chance. The dragon stretched its jaws wide, then struck straight down at him. Its teeth pierced through the old man, jerking his body like a mutt with a bone.

"*No!*" Naomi cried. "Elijah! What can we do?" She clung to me, shaking hard.

"We have to fight it." This creature was definitely and terribly real.

I aimed my gun and fired the laser into the dragon's body. It twisted and shrieked, but it was too late.

With a last snap of its head, it flung John high over our heads. His lifeless body crashed into the stones behind us. My breath froze.

Both of the priests were dead.

Naomi's face was ashen shock as tears began streaming down her cheeks. "Elijah!" she screamed. "Stop it!"

The dragon roared at me. The laser was a line connecting us, but this time the red beam did not pierce through. It was swallowed by the dark ribbons of smoke swirling around the dragon's body. I realized there was no way I could kill this thing.

The creature began to flap its wings and lift into the sky. It flew at us again. I tried to shield Naomi. The dragon was too fast. As it flashed by us, it swung its tail around my side and whipped it into Naomi.

Snap!

It sounded like her body broke. Then she was soaring through the air away from me. With a loud thud, she landed twenty feet away. Her body rolled to a stop in the shallowest water by the shore.

I sprinted to her. She was on her back, looking up at the sky. She was still breathing, barely.

"Everything is going to be okay," I lied.

"Elijah," she grimaced. "It wasn't…not like this."

"I'll get you to the boat now."

"No time," she gasped. "I'm dying."

"No." I spoke as if the word could change reality. "I

won't let you."

The dragon roared again in the distance. It almost sounded like laughter.

"Elijah, listen." She was motionless as tiny waves washed up against her body.

I put my hands on her cheeks and looked into her beautiful, distant eyes. "I'm listening. What?"

"You are chosen. A gift. You must see…prepare the way." She paused. It was too long a pause. I did not need our sync to tell me she was fading fast.

"Naomi!"

Her eyes saw me. "I love you…" she exhaled.

Then her eyes did not see me. They were blank.

"Wait, Naomi, wait! I love you."

She did not answer.

"No, please." A groan rose up from inside me. "*Nooo!*" I shouted. "*God, please, no…*take me!"

But her breaths had stopped. Her eyes froze, and she was right there, in my arms, dead.

42

My chest heaved as I knelt over Naomi's body.

I felt for a pulse and felt nothing. I laid my head on her chest, listening for anything. I heard nothing. I tried to turn on my precept, to check our sync. Nothing.

But I felt everything, deep in my core.

It was like a guillotine dropping on a thin thread, where the thread was a chance of a future together. How could I have held such hope for such frail twine? I should have known it would not hold in this chaos, much less against the dragon, the guillotine of my dreams.

As my emotions raged, the dragon and all else became nothing to me. My only reality was sobbing, tears falling on Naomi's motionless body.

I cried out again. "God," I pleaded. "If you bring her back, I'll believe. I promise I'll believe. Please…"

The dragon roared again. This time it sounded furious.

Over the creature's roaring, my cries, and the ocean sounds, I did not hear a man walk up behind me.

"Elijah." His voice was gentle but powerful. It was a new voice.

I turned to look at the man through my tears. I could hardly make out his face before he embraced me, holding me tight. His arms were strong. His scent overwhelmed me. It was like cedar, like fresh plowed earth, like a sea breeze. A few more sobs coursed through me and I became calm. The man released me but held my shoulders and looked at me. His eyes were like the sun, searing into me. I glanced away, unable to bear his gaze.

"Elijah," he said again.

I looked back at his face. He was just a normal man. The brightness was gone. His eyes were no longer like the sun. They were brown, just a plain, warm brown like his hair and beard.

"Naomi is waking," he said, stepping past me.

He reached down and touched her, almost the way Don had touched her. His hand pressed on her forehead.

I held my breath for a moment, with a glimmer of hope. But nothing happened.

He turned back to me. I could not find words to say. I must have looked dumb, my mouth ajar in disbelief, tear streaks down my face.

"Will you join us?" he asked. He clasped my shoulder again. Maybe he was one of the order, one of the twelve. Except there were only ten now.

"Who are you?" I asked.

A booming, crashing sound pulled my eyes away from him. I shivered as I saw the dragon land just above us on the hillside. It perched on a stone as big as a house. The dragon made it look like a pebble. It shrieked the worst sound I'd ever heard.

"Elijah," the man interrupted the sound. His voice hit me like cool water on a hot day.

I turned back to him. He seemed oblivious of the dragon. For some reason I'd hoped he could see it, too. But no, apparently only me.

"Will you prepare the way?" he asked.

"The way to where? What about the dragon?" He did not look at me like I was crazy. So maybe he could see something.

"I will defeat the dragon." He made it sound simple, like someone saying he would buy a loaf of bread.

"You are not even fighting," I pleaded. For some reason I felt like it would all be different if he were fighting.

"But I am and I will." He must have seen confusion on my face. "Time does not limit me."

Who said that kind of thing? I wondered if I was dreaming again, but I knew I wasn't. I glanced down. No ring was on the man's thumb. Who was he?

The dragon shrieked again and soared at us. The wind from its wings hit like a tornado's force, slamming me onto the hard ground and knocking the breath out of me.

I raised my eyes. The dragon's head was right in my face, staring at me. Its razor fangs almost smiled, but its slitted eyes filled with hate. Its neck coiled back. I was a dead man.

Boom!

The dragon struck at me, but it hit a wall. The wall was the man's word. I'd barely heard him say, "stop," but that's exactly what the creature had done.

The man was standing over me. While one hand was held in front of the dragon's head, he reached down with his other hand and lifted me to my knees.

"You are the second Elijah to come," he said, patient. This had to be a dream.

"Okay," I stammered. "But who are you?"

He touched my face. His hand was firm and hard, like a farmer's. "You will learn my name."

Time stood still as I looked into his eyes. They were like the sun again, but I let the brightness wash over me.

"Help is coming." He glanced down at Naomi. "Protect her."

I nodded, and then he looked to the dragon as it coiled back again and opened its mouth. Heat blared out, like a volcano erupting. Flames surged at my face. The inferno would burn me to cinders in an instant.

Then something flashed.

I do not know what caused the flash, but one second I cringed back, ready to be destroyed, and the next second a blinding white light erased everything around me. I was in the same position, but neither a dragon nor a man was anywhere to be seen.

I wanted it to have been a dream. But I knew it wasn't, because Naomi was by my side, lying still.

43

I sat in the shallow water and pulled Naomi's body into my arms. I held her close, and then I felt it.

A breath.

She was breathing. Unconscious but alive.

All sound was gone, as if I'd lost my hearing. My only sense was touch. I could feel Naomi's chest slowly rising and falling. I could feel the steady beat of her heart.

Then I felt an ocean breeze. It blew the earth's sound back into my mind. I heard the gentle lapping waves against the shore. I heard the cries of gulls above. I heard a distant, low humming.

That sound, the humming, was growing louder, or closer, or both. It drew my eyes away from Naomi's peaceful face to the west horizon, where the clear blue sky and sea melded together.

Something on the horizon looked like a cloud

approaching. It was a blur of white racing toward me faster than a cloud could blow. I realized it was a plane, some kind of jet, and the sound was the roar of its engine, lagging behind the flying object.

It closed the distance quickly. Suddenly it was hovering beside us like a giant disc. Its engines rotated down, blowing out blue-hot flames into the shallow water below. It lowered and, a few feet above the water's surface, the flames turned off and the disc dropped. Waves crashed out and the disc bobbed like a lifesaver's raft.

A door opened on the top. Two men climbed out, both wearing black body suits and helmets. A metal walkway slid out, and the men ran along it, leaping off the end into the waist-deep water. They charged toward us from there.

I sat waiting for them with Naomi in my arms.

As they reached us, the tinted glass masks of their helmets raised.

It was Chris. The same megachurch pastor Chris from DC. The other one was Patrick, ISA-7 Patrick. I pressed my eyes closed, then looked again. It was still Chris and Patrick.

"What happened?" Chris asked.

"I don't fully know," I said. "Why are you here?"

Patrick glared at me. "Naomi's vitals showed her heart stopped for several minutes." His face was pale against his black helmet. He had dark circles under his eyes. "What did you let happen to her?"

"I tried to save her." I held her tight against me. They had been monitoring her, probably tracking us. I didn't trust them. I was not letting her go.

"We're here to help." Chris held out his hand. "We'll get you to somewhere safe. Come with us."

I didn't move.

"You don't want to stay here," Patrick said. "Your precept is down. Another earthquake could come any time. You don't speak Greek."

"We're on your side," Chris added, somber. "We already lost two of our order here. Whatever happened, we have to get away. I promise, this is the best chance of protecting Naomi."

I chose my words carefully. "We were attacked."

"By what?" Patrick asked, scanning the hillside around us. "What could have killed John and Apollos in the space of five minutes? And where is Gregory? We lost the signal from his ring."

I remembered seeing Gregory, writhing on the ground after Naomi shot him. He had been alive when we left the cave. And how did Patrick know about John and Apollos? Could all of that information pass through their rings?

"Was it the dragon?" Chris asked.

My face must have given it away, because he nodded as if I had given him an answer.

"Patrick," he said, "take them back to the ship." He reached behind his back and pulled out a rifle. "I am going to search the area. If I'm not back in ten minutes, leave without me."

Patrick hesitated, then opened his mouth as if to protest.

"That's an order." Chris's tone eliminated the last of my doubts—this was no plain pastor. Their order had to be connected to ISA, the military, or something like that.

"Okay, ten minutes." Patrick turned to us. "You heard him, let's go."

I had little choice. "She stays within my reach at all times."

"Fine," said Chris.

"And you give me access to your network, so I can get my precept back online."

Chris gave me a hard look. "Elijah, we are on the same side." It was unclear whether that was a comfort or a threat. "You can use whatever we have, but you have to go, *now.*"

I stood with Naomi in my arms. Her limp body was heavy for my tired muscles.

Chris turned up the hillside, as Patrick led us to the disc plane. We walked on the thin metal ramp over the shallow water. The top of the disc had no identifying marks. There was a small opening with stairs leading down.

"You first," Patrick said.

"Is this all an ISA-7 operation?" I asked.

"You know I can't tell you that."

"Then I'm not going inside this plane." I studied his poker face. "Where are your loyalties—with ISA-7 or with this religious order?"

"It doesn't matter what I'm with," he said. "Get in, now."

Naomi suddenly stirred in my arms. "Water," she said

in the faintest voice.

"What did you say?" Patrick bent down closer to her.

I stepped back from him. "She wants water. You go first, we'll follow. Okay?"

"Fine." Patrick turned and climbed down the stairs.

I moved forward and heard Naomi's soft voice: "Elijah." Her eyes opened, gleaming like gold in the sun, then closed again peacefully.

I smiled and carried her into the plane.

44

With Naomi in my arms, I followed Patrick down a tube-shaped hall. Seams of metal and wire were forged into stripes of bright aluminum. I'd seen prototypes of this kind of plane, but I had no idea they already existed.

Patrick ducked into a round door near the back of the ship. Inside was a small room with a bed and medical equipment.

"Lay her down," said a woman's voice.

I looked around, then remembered where I was: back in the real world with technology. This was an automated medical system.

I did as the system said. Several devices and sensors began connecting to Naomi, while Patrick and I stood close by her side. I glanced around the room and noticed an uptake link for precepts in the back corner of the room.

"Is that where I can reboot?" I asked Patrick.

"Yes," he said, without taking his eyes off Naomi.

I went to the link and input my biometric codes. The ship's system began to reconnect my precept.

"Awaiting command," said V's voice in my mind a moment later. My senses came alive. My thinking sped up and focused. It was a bittersweet relief, like an addict going back to his drug after a month of detox. I realized there had been beauty in the freedom of my unenhanced senses. I had been liberated from the information, reports, and teaching that V had fed into me my entire life.

Now the information was back. My briefing screens showed destruction and devastation. It was just as Don Cristo had described it in his interview. Seven of the world's biggest cities were wiped out, including Rome. The U.S. lost San Francisco…completely. Smaller quakes rippled through every continent. The death count was estimated over two hundred million, and increasing. The UN had declared a global state of emergency and sent its drones and aid workers to the worst disaster areas.

V began to show a recording of President Cristo's latest speech. "Do not panic," he was saying. "The UN is prepared to keep the world safe. Our connections are secure. We will give you guidance about food and shelter. We have established direct connections with every activated precept. We are developing a new system to ensure everyone has what they need."

Blinking lights in the ship interrupted Cristo's speech. Pulsing data projected on the opposite side of Naomi's bed.

"Abnormal activity levels," diagnosed the medical

system's female voice.

"What kind?" I asked.

"Naomi Parish registers healthy measurements," the system explained, "but with twice the standard pulse rate and enhanced synaptic connections."

"You know what that means?" Patrick asked me.

"Not really, but it sounds like her mind and body are working in overdrive."

Naomi began to stir. Her eyes blinked open.

"You okay?" I asked.

"Much better," Naomi said, lying still. "I feel like I've just recovered from a terrible headache. It's like a vice was around my head, but now it's gone. Without that pressure, I feel like I could fly. My skin tingles. It feels, I don't know, almost like electricity is pulsing through my body."

"Maybe it is," Patrick said. "I think you're glowing."

Naomi sat halfway up, leaning on an elbow. She lifted her right hand. It was covered in dust and blood. I used a cloth to wipe away a layer of the grime. Her hand suddenly looked like it was basking in the sun. It seemed impossible for skin to look like that in the room's sterile light.

Naomi looked to me. "What happened?"

"We were attacked," I said.

"By the dragon?"

I nodded.

"I remember the woman, and…" She put her hand over her mouth, as if surprised by the memory. "We shot her…then something hit me…Oh God, what happened?"

Chris rushed into the room before I could answer. "I

confirmed it," he said. "There was only one survivor out there. John's and Apollos's bodies were gone." He made the sign of a cross over his chest. Everyone else in the room did the same. Everyone but me.

The loud thrum of the ship's jets turned on. I could feel the plane beginning to rise.

"We are leaving now," Chris said. He turned to Patrick. "Go to the cockpit, and send Bart back. He'll be desperate to talk to them."

Patrick frowned but obeyed and left the room.

Chris looked to me. "Is she okay?"

I nodded, my mind still trying to grasp that Bart was on this plane.

"Elijah saved me," Naomi said. "I knew he would."

"No, it wasn't..." I tried to say, but Chris interrupted me.

"You look amazing, like an angel," he uttered to Naomi. "Or like the hand of God touched you." He bowed down beside her and took her hand in his. "We thought we had lost you. What happened?"

"I told you," she smiled, "Elijah's vision came to be."

"Of course it did!" Bart declared as he charged into the room. Unlike Chris and Patrick with their black suits, Bart still wore an old brown robe. It was somehow comforting. "That's what I suspected all along. The boy is a seer— Elijah to come." His wild eyes fixed on me. "Aren't you?"

They all looked at me. I no longer doubted I'd seen things that they hadn't. If that made me a seer, so be it.

"That's what John told me," I said, "before he died."

"He's really dead? Tell me no." Bart turned to Chris, his giant chest beginning to heave in and out.

"We lost him, Bart." Chris put his arm on the huge man's shoulder. "And Apollos."

"No!" Bart fell to his knees, with his arms and head leaning by Naomi's side on the bed. His scruffy silver hair shook as he began to weep loudly. The ship lurched forward and hit the speed of sound.

Naomi put her hand on the back of Bart's head. "They are in a better place," she said.

He stopped crying and looked at her with his huge mouth hanging open.

"He's unbound, isn't he?" Bart asked.

Naomi shuddered as if someone rubbed a cube of ice down her neck. "Yes, Elijah saw the dragon. Don was there in Rome. I don't remember everything, but Elijah said he touched me."

"What did Don say?" Bart asked me. His eyes opened wider. "Is your precept connected?"

"Yes, why?"

"Shut if off!" he shouted. When I hesitated, he bellowed again, "*NOW!*"

He looked like he would tackle me if I didn't do it, so I did. My mind went bland again. I was the addict back in rehab.

Bart nodded, but then turned to Chris with desperation. "He'll find us now. They'll know where Elijah connected, and his trajectory. We have little time before an attack."

Chris glanced at me with sad eyes. "*How* did Don touch

her? Where?"

"Go ahead," said a familiar voice from the door. "Tell them, Elijah." It was a proper British voice.

"You're alive!" Bart stepped eagerly towards Gregory but suddenly froze.

The prince held a gun to Chris's head.

45

"Yes, Bart, I'm alive." Gregory pressed the gun into Chris's temple. "Chris found me and brought me here. Cheers, Chris, so very kind of you."

"Why would you?" Chris stammered.

"You'll see for yourself," Gregory said, looking to Naomi. "He's coming now to take back what's his."

"The dragon." Naomi's voice was soft, distant. She put her hands over her stomach. Fear was in her eyes. "I can *feel* his presence closing in on us."

"Indeed!" Gregory shoved Chris to the ground. "Did you really think you could stop my lord? He won't stop until all your order's leaders are dead—all twelve except for me."

"You are no threat to us, traitor," Bart growled.

"Has the old moose grown horns?" Gregory mocked.

"Put the gun down," Chris said. "You still have a

choice."

Gregory shook his head. "John said the same thing before we killed him."

A huge crash suddenly sent the room spinning. Red lights and alarm sounds blasted around us. I heard the sound of gunshots as I fell against Naomi's bed and clung fast to it.

When we stabilized, Gregory fled the room, chased by Bart. Chris was on the floor.

"Follow them," Chris commanded, and Patrick dashed out.

I looked down at Naomi. She nodded for me to go.

"Can you help me walk?" Chris asked Naomi. He winced and pressed his hands against his side. Had he been shot?

She rose from the bed. "Yes."

"Good." Chris turned to me. "She and I will go to the back, where there's an escape vessel. Help Bart and Patrick up front, but flee to us if things look grim."

I walked to the door, but stopped there. I had promised not to leave Naomi.

She came to my side and touched my face. "Go to them," she pleaded, "they need your vision. There will be more than a dragon this time. The sky will darken with his minions."

"Here." Chris held out his laser rifle to me. "Take this."

I took it. "Keep her safe."

Chris nodded. "Go, now."

I kissed Naomi's forehead. "I'll see you soon."

She nodded and said, "God bless," as I turned and ran toward the front of the plane.

The tight corridor was empty, but I kept the rifle raised. I had just reached the door at the end of the tube when the ship lurched again. I crashed to the floor, and the ship stabilized. My body groaned as I staggered back to my feet. I ignored the pain. I stepped forward and the door opened to a cockpit with walls of glass.

Standing in a triangle were Patrick, Bart, and Gregory. Patrick had his gun to Gregory's head. Gregory had his gun to Bart's head. Bart was holding a cross toward the window and mumbling something.

Outside was a vast desert. We were soaring over giant sand dunes. A hundred flying creatures dotted the sky around us. They looked like they were battling, wrestling for control of the air. But the largest creature seized my attention. It was the dragon. The dragon of my dreams, of Rome and of Patmos, and it was flying straight at us.

"Shoot him!" Bart shouted. "Patrick, fire now!"

"You shoot, and we all die," Gregory threatened. "Bart's the only thing keeping this ship in the air, and if you shoot, I shoot."

"Shoot him!" Bart shouted again. "Elijah will fly us out of here."

Gregory glanced at me, and the moment he did, Bart flung his huge mass at the prince. Patrick and I stood there, stunned, as Bart knocked away Gregory's gun and pummeled his face, like a killer silverback ape.

"The controls!" Bart commanded, pinning Gregory

down. The prince looked unconscious.

I dashed forward and grabbed the steering levers. The dragon's red eyes locked on me. We were on a collision course.

Patrick came to my side and readied to fire the ship's missiles. "Where is it?" he asked frantically. "Where do I shoot?"

But it was too late.

The dragon spun beneath the plane just as we collided. Claws that looked like iron cracked into the glass before us. The creature had grabbed our ship and was clinging to it as we soared ahead.

"Fly down!" Bart shoved me aside and seized the controls. He sent us spiraling down. The bottom of the ship clipped the top of an enormous sand dune, making us all fall forward, but the dragon's claws still clung to us.

As the plane rose again, the dragon slowly pulled itself up. Its face filled the cracked-glass view. It coiled back and struck before I could react. Its horned forehead slammed into the glass, shattering it into a million pieces. Wind tore into us. The creature roared out pure terror and fury.

Bart, scraped and bleeding, turned back to me. "Go!" he shouted. "Protect her, Elijah. Whatever you do, stay with her and keep her alive." He turned his desperate gaze to Patrick. "Go back to America with Chris. Serve the order first."

The priest turned away from us and jumped onto the dashboard of controls. He was holding a plain wooden cross, trying to look everywhere at once. He glanced back.

"I don't need to see him to believe. This date has long been planned." I could have sworn there was a grin hiding under his silver goatee. "Meet you on the other side. The plane's auto-pilot should give you enough time. Now go!"

The dragon struck again, crashing through the glass. It shrieked into the cockpit. Its jaws clamped around Bart and yanked him out of the plane. They spun down in the air, falling to the desert below.

All the other flying creatures were gone. The plane soared forward, but the alarms continued.

"Come on." I grabbed Patrick's arm and dragged him out of the cockpit and down the hall to the back of the ship.

"That was the dragon?" Terror laced Patrick's voice as he followed after me.

I did not stop to answer him. How had Naomi known it was coming? At least I wasn't the only one anymore. We could be crazy together.

"In here!" Chris shouted to us as we reached the back.

He and Naomi were seated in a tiny, round room with six chairs around the wall. Belts were tied around their chests and their waists.

"Sit down, buckle up," Chris said. He pointed at a screen on one of the walls. "Our last engine is about to blow. We have to eject."

Patrick and I did as he said.

"Where's Bart?" Naomi asked.

I met her eyes. "We lost him. The dragon attacked and took him. Last I saw, the two of them were crashing toward the desert. Bart was fighting on the way down."

"What about Gregory?" Chris asked.

"He's in the cockpit. Bart knocked him out."

"We have to leave him. He was already gone." Chris shook his head sadly. "Another member of the order is nearby and will protect us." He put his hand on a red lever by his side. Lights began to blink around us.

"System clear," said an automated voice. "Pull to eject."

Chris pulled the lever.

Our escape pod shot up into the air like a rocket.

I glanced out one of the small windows and felt like I was looking at earth from outer space. The outline of northwest Africa was below us. Our ascent began to slow and then we were drifting down like a hot air balloon losing heat.

When I turned back from the window, Naomi was watching me. "We'll be safe where we're going," she said.

"Somewhere in Africa?"

She nodded.

"The wilderness in eastern Morocco," said Chris. "We'd been planning to make a stop here on our way to Jerusalem, but with our ship intact. We'll have to find another way home."

"Won't the dragon follow us?" I asked.

"I doubt it, thanks to Bart." Chris looked out of the

pod, to the west. "The plane is on track to crash somewhere in the Atlantic. No one will know where we ejected, but I timed it so we'd drop in the right spot. We've turned our precepts off. Don and the others won't be able to track us."

Really? I thought. Maybe that was true for Don, but whatever the dragon was, I doubted it needed a tracker.

"But they'll know we're in this region." Patrick rubbed his eyes while he spoke. "The dragon...or whatever that invisible thing was...it will come back for us."

Chris handed Patrick a wet cloth. "Wipe your face, Patrick. You need to pull it together."

Patrick sighed as he pressed his face into the cloth and held it there. He seemed older, less innocent, when he pulled the cloth away. "I never thought we'd lose Bart." He gazed out the window. "How am I going to explain the lost plane to ISA-7?"

"You'll come up with something. Maybe you can blame me," Naomi suggested. "The Captain and Aisha already suspected my true loyalties were elsewhere. I don't think they know yet that you're affiliated with the order."

Naomi's voice had pulled Patrick's gaze away from the window. He looked on her with wonder.

"What happened to you?" he asked. "You were dead."

She glanced at me and shrugged.

Patrick turned to me. "What happened, Eli?"

"I don't know." I considered telling them about the man, whoever that guy was who had touched Naomi's forehead just like Don. But I wasn't ready to face any more questions, not yet. "One second she was dead," I said, "then she was alive. I don't know how to explain it."

"He's lying," Patrick said, swiveling his head from Chris to Naomi and back, as if looking for help.

"It's clear you're hiding something," Chris said to me, "but that's okay for now. There's a purpose for this. Maybe we aren't supposed to know." He smiled—his real smile. "Can't you tell us anything else?"

I shook my head.

"It's a miracle…God's healing touch," Naomi volunteered. "We never fight alone."

Our group fell into quiet then, rocking from one side to the other as the pod drifted down. I watched out the window as the ground rose to meet us. After several minutes, we touched down in a valley amidst barren, rocky hills stretching as far as I could see. We each gathered up supplies from the pod and then clambered out. The sun was low on the horizon. Another long day.

Chris led us out of the valley, heading north. He was slowed by the wound at his side, but he continued through the pain. "I'll be fine," was all he said when Naomi asked about it.

The land was harsh around us. A few shrubs clung to the sandy soil between rocks, but there was no sign of water. We had been hiking about an hour and were on a hilltop when we saw a figure in the distance. It was someone on a camel, with a trail of camels behind him. They were just cresting the next hill and making their way toward us.

"That should be him." Chris sounded weak. "Come on, just a little further."

We began descending the next hill, just as the other man descended the opposite hill. It was almost dark when we met. The man had a dense beard and a white cloth tied around his head.

"Jacques!" Chris greeted him.

"You arrive late." He held open his arms in welcome. His accent was French. "I bring Camille's stew, but now it is cold. Perhaps we camp here. What do you say, my brother?"

"I say I've never been happier to see you." Chris failed to hide the pain in his voice.

"You're hurt." The man went to Chris's side.

"It's nothing. A stigmata of service."

"A heavy word." The man helped Chris to sit on the ground. "But these are heavy times, eh? Who are these friends you bring to my desert?"

Chris motioned to us. "This is Patrick, my assistant, and this is Elijah, a seer."

The man studied me with a slanted grin. He was younger than I had expected, about Chris's age. "We have been waiting for you," he said to me.

"And I am Naomi." She stepped to my side and pulled back the cowl that had been blocking the wind and sun from her face.

The man gasped, "*Mon Dieu!*" He made the cross over his chest. He bowed, took Naomi's hand, and kissed it. "I am Jacques Guillaume. It is an honor, *femme revêtue du soleil.*"

"What does that mean?" Patrick asked. My rough translation was something like *woman coated in sun*. I figured it made sense—her face shone in the fading daylight.

"Why did you not tell me?" Jacques asked Chris, ignoring Patrick's question.

"I just found out myself," Chris said. "We must consult with the order as soon as possible. We need to figure out what happened, and what's coming next. It's going to be hard without Bart."

The man's body went rigid. "Without Bart?"

Chris nodded. "We lost him, Jacques."

Jacques pressed his eyes closed and leaned his head back, facing the sky. "Heavy times indeed."

Chris put his hand on the man's shoulder. "We should wait to speak more of this in private. How about some of that stew?"

"Yes, yes." Jacques stood, eyeing Naomi. "We must get you rest. As I say, this is a good place to make camp. At first light we go to my home. Camille will feed you. We have stew, we have wine, and then we talk more. "

47

Jacques began barking orders to us, half in French, half in English. He sounded like a drill sergeant, setting us tasks of gathering sparse brush, laying out beds, building a fire, and feeding the camels. While we followed his orders, he tended to Chris's wound.

Once the small fire was burning, Jacques heated the stew and served each of us. It was just lentils with some spice like saffron, but my starving belly found it delicious. I ate quickly and said goodnight to the others.

I went to my make-shift bed and laid down, exhausted. I could barely keep my eyes open. Was it just yesterday morning Naomi and I landed in Rome?

I looked up at the sky. The moon was a pale sliver, and the stars were radiant. There were more than I had ever seen. Each one was like a door with a dream behind it. I did not want to walk through any more doors like that.

"Beautiful, aren't they?" Naomi laid down on her back beside me. Her bed was next to mine, and a safe distance from the others. There were perks to being assigned the task of setting up beds.

"Not as beautiful as you." The starlight made her skin turn a rich, silver hue.

She laughed. "I'm glad you haven't lost your sense of humor." She was quiet for a moment, her body still. "We've seen a lot. We've lost a lot."

"I know, I'm sorry."

"It's not your fault." She turned on her side and looked at me. Her eyes made my breath freeze. They were like Jezebel's, except they were the sun instead of magma. "You saved me."

"I, no…"

"I know why you don't want to tell the others, but please, tell me what happened." She reached out and put her hand against my cheek. It thawed my resistance.

"There was a man. He came to us out of nowhere."

"When?"

"After you died. The dragon was still there, but the man stopped it. He touched you, like this." I pressed my hand on her forehead. It was smooth and warm.

"What did the man look like?"

"He was normal, like anyone, like me. He had brown hair and a beard, nothing special, except…"

"Except what?"

"His eyes," I began. "Sometimes they glowed, kind of like yours."

"Did you talk to him?"

I nodded. "I asked him his name. He told me I would learn it. He told me that help was coming. Then he was gone, and so was the dragon. I ran back to you, and you were alive."

"So it was a miracle," she whispered, with a look of awe. "What else did he say?"

I thought back through my blurred memories. It was still hard without V. "He asked me to prepare the way. I don't know what that meant. He told me to protect you. Do you have any idea who it was?"

She smiled at me. "You saw him, not me. This doesn't seem like something I should guess about."

"What, was he some augmented ISA prototype, with some super-secret precept?"

"No," she laughed lightly. The sound helped my body relax. "I don't think he had anything to do with ISA. How did he stop the dragon?"

"He just told it to stop, and it did." That sounded even more ridiculous than it had seemed in the moment.

But Naomi nodded as if she understood. "He may be the one you have to prepare the way for, but that is for you to decide. Whoever he was, I'm glad he's on our side."

We were quiet then, just staring at each other. The camp was quiet, too. The still of the night made my eyes heavier.

"What's coming next?" I wondered aloud.

"I don't know, Elijah." She took my hand in hers. "But you'll stay with me, right?"

"Always," I said, meeting her smile. I felt like God had answered my plea to save her. The least I could do was try to keep her safe. "Do you remember the last thing you said to me, before you died?" I remembered too well. It was, *I love you*, but had she really said it, and meant it? People could say anything on a deathbed.

She thought for a moment. "I said you are chosen, that you must use your gift to see, right?"

"Yeah," I said, hope sinking inside me, "it was something like that." I squeezed her hand in mine. "Don't die again, okay?"

"I won't if you won't let me," she teased.

I nodded. "Deal. Goodnight, Naomi."

"Goodnight."

We drifted to sleep soon after that. I would have paid a fortune for a dream pill, but those things don't grow in deserts. And so the visions came.

My mom was standing beside my dad. His hand was at the back of her neck, hidden behind her black curls. She smiled up at him, and he smiled down at her. I'd forgotten he could smile like that.

They were standing in a temple. I could see through the walls. I could see New York City around them. I could see an enormous wave crashing toward the skyscrapers. Its frothy crest reached nearly half way up the towers.

Suddenly I was between my mom and my dad, holding their legs and looking up at them. I knew the wave was coming, but they didn't. Or at least my dad didn't. My mom looked at me and mouthed a silent prayer. My dad just stared at her, oblivious to everything around us.

When the wave hit, my dad fell. The building collapsed over him and he was trapped under the water. But my mom and I just floated out. She rose like a balloon, drifting above the city. I was the little boy holding the string that dangled from her as we rose above the buildings that peeked out of the swirling water. The whole city was submerged.

My mom held out her hand to me. I took it and she scooped me into her arms, as if I was a baby.

"This isn't real," I said to her.

She looked lovingly into my eyes and said, "You must learn to see the truth in your dreams. They will pursue you until you heed them. The word is living and active, piercing to the division of soul and of spirit."

"Does that mean he's dead?"

She nodded sadly. "He's in the space between now. He loves you, Elijah, just as I do."

"But you are dead, too." Despite my words, she looked more alive than I could imagine. She looked even more alive than my memories of her.

"You have seen the dead return to life," she said.

"Naomi?"

She smiled and nodded. "The woman clothed with the sun. You must protect them both."

"Who else?"

Suddenly others were around my mom. They had wings. They looked like the creatures that had fought in the sky when our ship was going down. They looked like angels. One of them put his hand on my mom's shoulder.

"I have to go now," she told me.

"No, please." I tried to cling to her, but my pudgy infant arms were too weak. "I need you."

"I will watch over you," she said, "but you must learn to fly on your own."

Then she let go of me, and I fell. I soared straight down, toward the drowned city below. But now the wave was retreating. The froth pulled back, revealing devastated steel and pavement below.

I fell so fast. The wind whipped at me. I knew I would die when I landed. My own mother had let me go. She had let me fall, and I was going to die.

Just before I hit the ground, I woke up.

48

Naomi woke me at dawn the next morning. I could get used to her face being the first thing I saw every day. Its radiance burned away some residue of my dream.

Next came more commands from Jacques. I fumbled through the tasks, clueless about packing up a camp, especially without my precept. Packing was easier, though, than riding a camel. Jacques said my camel's name was *Grabuge*—"trouble."

Our camels formed a line following Jacques over miles and miles of rocky scrubland. As we rode, Jacques updated us on Don's latest maneuvers since the earthquakes. He'd ordered a link between every precept and the UN's global satellite system. He'd said it was just temporary, for safety and tracking purposes following the disasters. He'd called for the world's leaders to gather to discuss how to solve their conflicts in unity. He'd promised a new hope for mankind, through something he called the Omega Project. No one, not even the order, had guesses about what that project would be.

After a while, Chris and Jacques rode slightly ahead to talk in private. That left me with Naomi and Patrick. We hardly spoke, which suited me just fine. It was taking enough effort just to hold onto *Grabuge*. By the time the sun reached its peak, my entire body ached as the camel swayed and jerked his way forward.

The camel had tried to bite me a dozen times. After I'd punched him in the face once, we'd come to a delicate truce. I gripped the reins harder. I wouldn't dare fall off. If I did, *Grabuge* would bite me for sure, and he'd probably spit on me for good measure.

"There's our oasis!" Jacques finally announced from ahead, as we crested another hill.

In the valley below there were three palm trees in a cluster. Just three.

We followed Jacques down the steep slope. As we rode closer, I noticed a few low canvas buildings were scattered around the palms. They were nearly invisible from a distance.

A woman came out to greet us. She had long black hair and bronzed skin. She wore leather-strapped sandals, loose-fitting khaki pants, and a white tunic. In the wind, the light fabric blew against her slim body. Her face was gorgeous, but showed no hint of a smile. She looked like she could be walking from her vacation villa to the beach, instead of from some tents in a desert to a caravan of filthy travelers.

She introduced herself as Camille, but she spoke not a word of English. She fawned over Jacques, Chris, and Naomi. She ignored Patrick and me.

Jacques led us toward one of the tents. A pot of spicy-smelling stew was simmering over a fire outside.

"Lentil stew." Jacques gestured toward the pot and smiled at us. "Camille makes the finest stew within a five-day ride. The secret is the tarragon." He picked up a stack of bowls and spoons. "Here, take, we eat inside."

Each of us filled a bowl and went into the tent. The six of us sat in a circle on a bright-patterned rug. The stew was the same as the night before, only warmer.

Camille was the last to join us. "*Quand partez-vous?*" Her question sounded like amused contempt. Maybe she was a movie star gone into early retirement.

"*Dans une heure,*" Chris answered. His accent sounded flawless, but who was I to know? He looked to Patrick. "You'll come with me."

Patrick nodded. "But what about Naomi?"

"*Avec-vous fait?*" Camille challenged him.

"English," Jacques pleaded at her side. "My love, a little honor for our guests, yes?" He rubbed her shoulder gently. "Remember, their precepts are off."

"*Oui,*" she answered. "You will not take the girl, or whichever boy did it. *Bien?*" The woman was looking at me accusingly. What did she think I had done?

"Okay," Chris said. "Jacques will lead Patrick and me to the closest town. From there we will make our way back to our country. We'll be seen as we travel. Our enemies will be searching the area. By dividing, we might protect Naomi and Elijah here. You will keep them safe?"

"*Oui.*" Camille turned to me. She studied me like a teacher studies a naughty boy. "*Si il l'a fait.*" A devious little grin touched her beautiful face.

I did what? She seemed to know something I didn't.

"How long before you come back for us?" Naomi asked.

"I don't know," Chris said to her. "It may be a long time. As much as I'd like your help with our mission, your safety is the most important thing. Jacques and Camille can protect you here. We'll maintain an encrypted connection to them. Communicate rarely to avoid risking discovery, but signal any danger."

Naomi nodded but looked uncertain.

"We have a good home," Jacques assured her. He rubbed the salt-and-pepper stubble on his chin. "We can learn from you more of what has happened in these recent days."

"And you can learn from us," Camille added, again with a conspiratorial tone.

The talk turned to logistics of travel and communication as we finished our stew. In short order, Chris and Patrick said their goodbyes and left with Jacques. Chris seemed above all in a hurry to be gone. Maybe "our enemies," as he'd called them, were closer than I thought.

After they departed, Naomi, Camille, and I sat outside at the base of one of the palm trees. Camille began to ask us innocent questions about our past. We had been talking only half an hour when Naomi's face went ashen.

"What is it?" I asked her.

"I feel something…I don't know…dark." She looked to the sky, and as if on cue, the dragon's long sinuous body flew overhead in the direction the men had gone. Its giant shadow snaked over the oasis without pausing.

"What are you looking at?" Camille asked us.

"I'm not sure," Naomi muttered, "Elijah?"

"It's the dragon," I said, this time with full conviction of what I'd seen. "It just flew past—there." I pointed to it on the horizon. "It seemed to be looking ahead, instead of searching around us."

"The ancient serpent unbound," Naomi added.

"Quiet. Say no more." Camille studied Naomi and me with a look of concern on her face.

Long after the dragon had disappeared, Naomi shuddered and put her hand to her belly. "I don't feel well."

"I can understand that," said Camille.

"You can?" Naomi asked.

"I have a son, myself," she said. "Haven't you heard morning sickness is not confined to the mornings?"

"What?" I blurted out.

"That's impossible," Naomi said.

"You tell that to God," Camille said, "and to your boyfriend." She looked at me accusingly again.

"No, really," I said, "it's impossible."

"Look at her, seer."

I did, and Naomi's scared face shined at me.

"You see," Camille said, "she's pregnant. Aren't you girl?"

Naomi looked down at her waist. She put her hands over her stomach, and quietly began to cry.

END OF BOOK ONE

Ω

AUTHOR PAGE

Want to know who the baby's father is? You'll learn that and much more in the next book of the trilogy: *Clothed With The Sun*. Visit **www.jbsimmons.com** for a free preview.

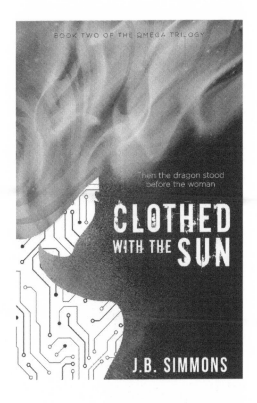

J.B. Simmons lives outside Washington, DC, with his wife and three little kids. He writes before dawn and runs all day. His secret fuel: coffee and leftover juice boxes. Learn more at www.jbsimmons.com.

ACKNOWLEDGMENTS

Thanks to Lindsay for always pushing me to be better. Thanks to my family and friends for providing the love and support from which art can grow. Thanks to the Neukomms, because the spark of this idea came during a visit to their book-filled home. Thanks to the fantastic beta-readers: Anne, Danny, Gigi, Grace, Kimberly, Jean, Lindsay, Michael, Nate, Rebekah, Ronnie, and Ryan. *Unbound* would not be what it is without them.

OTHER WORKS BY J.B. SIMMONS

LIGHT IN THE GLOAMING
BREAKING THE GLOAMING

In the *Gloaming* books, J.B. Simmons weaves political philosophy into fantasy, like *A Game of Thrones* with a C.S. Lewis twist. The characters champion history's great thinkers, from Machiavelli to Locke to Nietzsche, and bring them to battle, even in the darkest of underground cities: The Gloaming.

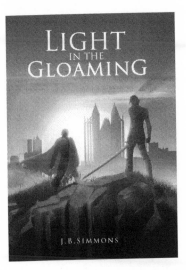

"Tightly crafted . . . a real triumph to creative literature and well deserving of its stars."
Sara Bain, Ivy Moon Press

"A great mix of fantasy, adventure, and allegory." Sunshine Somerville, author, *The Kota Series*

"The characters were outstanding . . . The story was excellent . . . [E]very part of the world is more brilliant in the way the author describes it."
Two Reads Blog

Available on Amazon. Preview at www.jbsimmons.com.